HER LAST

FEAR

(A Rachel Gift Mystery—Book Four)

BLAKE PIERCE

Blake Pierce

Blake Pierce is the USA Today bestselling author of the RILEY PAGE mystery series, which includes seventeen books. Blake Pierce is also the author of the MACKENZIE WHITE mystery series, comprising fourteen books; of the AVERY BLACK mystery series, comprising six books; of the KERI LOCKE mystery series, comprising five books; of the MAKING OF RILEY PAIGE mystery series, comprising six books; of the KATE WISE mystery series, comprising seven books; of the CHLOE FINE psychological suspense mystery, comprising six books; of the JESSE HUNT psychological suspense thriller series, comprising twenty four books; of the AU PAIR psychological suspense thriller series, comprising three books; of the ZOE PRIME mystery series, comprising six books; of the ADELE SHARP mystery series, comprising fifteen books, of the EUROPEAN VOYAGE cozy mystery series, comprising four books; of the new LAURA FROST FBI suspense thriller, comprising nine books (and counting); of the new ELLA DARK FBI suspense thriller, comprising eleven books (and counting); of the A YEAR IN EUROPE cozy mystery series, comprising nine books, of the AVA GOLD mystery series, comprising six books (and counting); of the RACHEL GIFT mystery series, comprising six books (and counting); of the VALERIE LAW mystery series, comprising six books (and counting); and of the PAIGE KING mystery series, comprising six books (and counting).

An avid reader and lifelong fan of the mystery and thriller genres, Blake loves to hear from you, so please feel free to visit www.blakepierceauthor.com to learn more and stay in touch.

BOOKS BY BLAKE PIERCE

PAIGE KING MYSTERY SERIES
THE GIRL HE PINED (Book #1)
THE GIRL HE CHOSE (Book #2)
THE GIRL HE TOOK (Book #3)
THE GIRL HE WISHED (Book #4)
THE GIRL HE CROWNED (Book #5)
THE GIRL HE WATCHED (Book #6)

VALERIE LAW MYSTERY SERIES
NO MERCY (Book #1)
NO PITY (Book #2)
NO FEAR (Book #3)
NO SLEEP (Book #4)
NO QUARTER (Book #5)
NO CHANCE (Book #6)

RACHEL GIFT MYSTERY SERIES
HER LAST WISH (Book #1)
HER LAST CHANCE (Book #2)
HER LAST HOPE (Book #3)
HER LAST FEAR (Book #4)
HER LAST CHOICE (Book #5)
HER LAST BREATH (Book #6)

AVA GOLD MYSTERY SERIES
CITY OF PREY (Book #1)
CITY OF FEAR (Book #2)
CITY OF BONES (Book #3)
CITY OF GHOSTS (Book #4)
CITY OF DEATH (Book #5)
CITY OF VICE (Book #6)

A YEAR IN EUROPE
A MURDER IN PARIS (Book #1)
DEATH IN FLORENCE (Book #2)
VENGEANCE IN VIENNA (Book #3)

A FATALITY IN SPAIN (Book #4)

ELLA DARK FBI SUSPENSE THRILLER
GIRL, ALONE (Book #1)
GIRL, TAKEN (Book #2)
GIRL, HUNTED (Book #3)
GIRL, SILENCED (Book #4)
GIRL, VANISHED (Book 5)
GIRL ERASED (Book #6)
GIRL, FORSAKEN (Book #7)
GIRL, TRAPPED (Book #8)
GIRL, EXPENDABLE (Book #9)
GIRL, ESCAPED (Book #10)
GIRL, HIS (Book #11)

LAURA FROST FBI SUSPENSE THRILLER
ALREADY GONE (Book #1)
ALREADY SEEN (Book #2)
ALREADY TRAPPED (Book #3)
ALREADY MISSING (Book #4)
ALREADY DEAD (Book #5)
ALREADY TAKEN (Book #6)
ALREADY CHOSEN (Book #7)
ALREADY LOST (Book #8)
ALREADY HIS (Book #9)

EUROPEAN VOYAGE COZY MYSTERY SERIES
MURDER (AND BAKLAVA) (Book #1)
DEATH (AND APPLE STRUDEL) (Book #2)
CRIME (AND LAGER) (Book #3)
MISFORTUNE (AND GOUDA) (Book #4)
CALAMITY (AND A DANISH) (Book #5)
MAYHEM (AND HERRING) (Book #6)

ADÈLE SHARP MYSTERY SERIES
LEFT TO DIE (Book #1)
LEFT TO RUN (Book #2)
LEFT TO HIDE (Book #3)
LEFT TO KILL (Book #4)
LEFT TO MURDER (Book #5)

LEFT TO ENVY (Book #6)
LEFT TO LAPSE (Book #7)
LEFT TO VANISH (Book #8)
LEFT TO HUNT (Book #9)
LEFT TO FEAR (Book #10)
LEFT TO PREY (Book #11)
LEFT TO LURE (Book #12)
LEFT TO CRAVE (Book #13)
LEFT TO LOATHE (Book #14)
LEFT TO HARM (Book #15)

THE AU PAIR SERIES
ALMOST GONE (Book#1)
ALMOST LOST (Book #2)
ALMOST DEAD (Book #3)

ZOE PRIME MYSTERY SERIES
FACE OF DEATH (Book#1)
FACE OF MURDER (Book #2)
FACE OF FEAR (Book #3)
FACE OF MADNESS (Book #4)
FACE OF FURY (Book #5)
FACE OF DARKNESS (Book #6)

A JESSIE HUNT PSYCHOLOGICAL SUSPENSE SERIES
THE PERFECT WIFE (Book #1)
THE PERFECT BLOCK (Book #2)
THE PERFECT HOUSE (Book #3)
THE PERFECT SMILE (Book #4)
THE PERFECT LIE (Book #5)
THE PERFECT LOOK (Book #6)
THE PERFECT AFFAIR (Book #7)
THE PERFECT ALIBI (Book #8)
THE PERFECT NEIGHBOR (Book #9)
THE PERFECT DISGUISE (Book #10)
THE PERFECT SECRET (Book #11)
THE PERFECT FAÇADE (Book #12)
THE PERFECT IMPRESSION (Book #13)
THE PERFECT DECEIT (Book #14)
THE PERFECT MISTRESS (Book #15)

THE PERFECT IMAGE (Book #16)
THE PERFECT VEIL (Book #17)
THE PERFECT INDISCRETION (Book #18)
THE PERFECT RUMOR (Book #19)
THE PERFECT COUPLE (Book #20)
THE PERFECT MURDER (Book #21)
THE PERFECT HUSBAND (Book #22)
THE PERFECT SCANDAL (Book #23)
THE PERFECT MASK (Book #24)

CHLOE FINE PSYCHOLOGICAL SUSPENSE SERIES
NEXT DOOR (Book #1)
A NEIGHBOR'S LIE (Book #2)
CUL DE SAC (Book #3)
SILENT NEIGHBOR (Book #4)
HOMECOMING (Book #5)
TINTED WINDOWS (Book #6)

KATE WISE MYSTERY SERIES
IF SHE KNEW (Book #1)
IF SHE SAW (Book #2)
IF SHE RAN (Book #3)
IF SHE HID (Book #4)
IF SHE FLED (Book #5)
IF SHE FEARED (Book #6)
IF SHE HEARD (Book #7)

THE MAKING OF RILEY PAIGE SERIES
WATCHING (Book #1)
WAITING (Book #2)
LURING (Book #3)
TAKING (Book #4)
STALKING (Book #5)
KILLING (Book #6)

RILEY PAIGE MYSTERY SERIES
ONCE GONE (Book #1)
ONCE TAKEN (Book #2)
ONCE CRAVED (Book #3)

ONCE LURED (Book #4)
ONCE HUNTED (Book #5)
ONCE PINED (Book #6)
ONCE FORSAKEN (Book #7)
ONCE COLD (Book #8)
ONCE STALKED (Book #9)
ONCE LOST (Book #10)
ONCE BURIED (Book #11)
ONCE BOUND (Book #12)
ONCE TRAPPED (Book #13)
ONCE DORMANT (Book #14)
ONCE SHUNNED (Book #15)
ONCE MISSED (Book #16)
ONCE CHOSEN (Book #17)

MACKENZIE WHITE MYSTERY SERIES
BEFORE HE KILLS (Book #1)
BEFORE HE SEES (Book #2)
BEFORE HE COVETS (Book #3)
BEFORE HE TAKES (Book #4)
BEFORE HE NEEDS (Book #5)
BEFORE HE FEELS (Book #6)
BEFORE HE SINS (Book #7)
BEFORE HE HUNTS (Book #8)
BEFORE HE PREYS (Book #9)
BEFORE HE LONGS (Book #10)
BEFORE HE LAPSES (Book #11)
BEFORE HE ENVIES (Book #12)
BEFORE HE STALKS (Book #13)
BEFORE HE HARMS (Book #14)

AVERY BLACK MYSTERY SERIES
CAUSE TO KILL (Book #1)
CAUSE TO RUN (Book #2)
CAUSE TO HIDE (Book #3)
CAUSE TO FEAR (Book #4)
CAUSE TO SAVE (Book #5)
CAUSE TO DREAD (Book #6)

KERI LOCKE MYSTERY SERIES

CHAPTER ONE

Theresa had no idea what she'd been thinking. When Derek had asked if she wanted to go for a hike, she should have known he had something extreme in mind. Eager to please, she'd agreed to it. She was in good shape but hated the dry New Mexico heat. It was a beautiful state, and she was glad she'd moved out here; but Jesus, the heat could be unbearable at times.

Derek was hiking just ahead of her as they made their way through one of the many trails along the Chihuahuan Desert. They were headed to something called Little Squaretop, a feature along this trail that was supposed to provide an amazing view of the desert. But the hike was six and a half miles long through this God forsaken desert. For people that were accustomed to hiking, it was supposed to take about five hours. And Theresa wasn't sure there was any view on the planet that was worth that sort of torture.

Then again, she thought Derek might be taking her to such a view for a very specific reason. They'd been dating for almost two years now, and at twenty-seven years of age, she wasn't exactly getting any younger.

As they trudged along with open desert and craggy rock formations to both sides, Derek looked back to her. "How you doing back there?"

"Just great."

He smiled at her, readjusting the small backpack he was wearing on his muscular, tan shoulders. She took a few quick steps to catch up to him. They'd both broken a slight sweat and the pressing heat was not going to let up anytime soon.

"We're about halfway there, right?" she said.

"Maybe a bit more than that." He frowned apologetically as he looked at the trail just ahead of them. "Sorry, babe. I really didn't think it would be this hot. There's usually a really nice breeze that cuts through here."

"It's okay. You just keep in mind that if I pass out from heat stroke, you're going to have to walk back carrying my limp body."

He reached out and took her hand. "I don't quite think it'll come to that."

"At the risk of sounding like a wuss, I think I would like to sit down sometime soon. Maybe for just like five minutes or so. Is that okay?"

"Of course."

She could tell that he felt bad about her being uncomfortable. But really, what else had he expected? She supposed he found it cute that she was struggling so much. *At least I'm getting a tan,* she thought. *And this walk is going to count for every single bit of my cardio this week.*

They continued up the trail as it made a slight yet continual rise. Theresa looked to her right and saw that there was already a very nice view starting to present itself. The desert, she supposed, was very much like the Appalachian Mountains near where she'd grown up. Catch either of them at a certain angle or a certain light and they could be breathtaking.

"Think you can make it over there?" Derek asked, pointing ahead and to the right. There was a little raised section of rock protruding from the desert ground. It was only about three hundred feet further ahead, but it was off to the right and slightly off the beaten trail. It looked back out the way they came, and she thought it might provide just a small taste of the view that was to come once they finally reached the summit of Little Squaretop.

"Yeah, I think I can manage that," she said, putting some dramatic flair into just how tired she was.

She regretted the slight mockery when the ground seemed to suddenly change direction, heading in a harsh arc upwards. She really had to dig her ankles in, her knees groaning with the effort. It flattened back out gradually just before Derek led them off into harder dirt and some very sad-looking scrub brush.

They settled down on the rock he'd pointed out. Theresa tried to hide the instant relief to her ankles and knees. She stretched her legs out, relishing the feel of it.

"I do appreciate you doing this with me," Derek said, kissing her on the cheek.

The way he looked at her as he pulled away made her pretty certain that the hike was going to end with Derek on a knee, looking up to her with a ring in his hand. She smiled her best casual smile and shrugged. "I'm a big girl," she said. "This isn't so bad."

"So do you think I could talk you into camping soon?"

"No," she said. "That's where I draw the line. Why am I going to waltz out into the desert and pretend to be homeless for a night? It makes no sense. It makes…"

She stopped here as she looked beyond Derek. She was looking to the desert floor roughly seventy feet below them. More specifically, she was looking at a rock very similar to the one she and Derek were sitting on. It was just barely in her line of view; if she'd been sitting back another six inches on the rock, she may not have seen it at all.

"What?" Derek asked. "What is it?"

She opened her mouth to vocalize what she was seeing but her eyes didn't seem to fully understand what it was trying to process.

Blood. Lots of blood. A bare, slender leg. A hand and the lower portion of an arm, the rest of the arm blocked off by her angle and the rocky terrain between her and the grisly sight.

And buzzards, too. My God, buzzards, picking at that bare leg, huddled around and—

"Theresa?"

"A body," she said, pointing to what she was seeing. The word felt like a curse coming out.

Derek turned and saw it, too. "My God," he gasped.

They both stood slowly and walked closer to the edge of their little rock outcropping. From there, the angle and obstructions were gone. Theresa now had no problems seeing the full sight. The body was far enough away so that they were spared some of the gore, but close enough for Theresa to fill in the blanks. Blood everywhere. A woman, naked, most of her left side butchered and bloody. Her blonde hair spread out around the rock like an exploded star. A cavernous hole where her heart was—or should be.

The buzzards, feeding.

Somehow, Theresa knew the woman's eyes were open, looking right up at them.

The scream started to rise up out of Theresa's throat before she knew it was there. But when it came rushing up her throat and out into the air, it felt justified. Her scream tore out across the open desert, sending the buzzards skyward, their beaks slick and red from the meal down below.

CHAPTER TWO

Rachel had only been to a single doctor after getting her initial diagnosis. But that visit had been more than enough for her to get a read on how doctors presented themselves when they were about to dole out bad news. From what she could tell, there was a notable effort to make sure the brow wasn't creased at all and that the corners of their mouths remained stationary and straight—not drooping to create a frown and certainly not ticked upwards to indicate any sort of happiness.

She saw that now as Dr. Emerson pulled his little rolling stool over to where Rachel sat in a very basic, cushioned chair. Visible effort to keep the mouth and brow featureless, an air of seriousness following across the room like a little cartoon rain cloud.

Rachel had come in last week for a series of tests—all rather simple and non-invasive. She'd come at Jack's suggestion, trying out the specialist he'd suggested. And now here she was, back in the same office but the room had a different feel now. The nurses and assistants were a thing of the past. Now it was just Rachel and Dr. Emerson. This was, she supposed, the endgame.

Emerson seemed to know it, too. He looked her in the eyes with the compassion of a skilled and well-practiced doctor. "Mrs. Gift, I wish I had better news, but all of the tests and scans just don't offer us any good news."

Rachel wasn't sure how she felt about the sense of indifference that came over her. She had come in last week without expecting much of anything. She'd been *expecting* this answer. But still, shouldn't she be disappointed? Maybe even just a little?

She shrugged and tried to offer a resigned smile.

"The tumor, as I'm sure you know, is in a place that simply won't allow us to operate. I even considered maybe suggesting a specialist in Canada, out of Quebec, that is brilliant with the removal of risky tumors. But I don't know that he'd even offer much hope. Now, I can contact him if you like. I'm sure he'd at least—"

"No, that's okay." She'd seen the doubt in his eyes before he'd even finished the comment. "I knew what to expect when I came. I knew it was a longshot."

4

Emerson nodded, his graying black hair falling slightly over his still-unmoving brow. "I think maybe it's a good thing you came in. There's nothing at all wrong with having a bit of hope."

She found the comment vaguely funny. Hope. She wondered if he'd be talking about hope if he knew some of the other details of her life— about a husband that walked out on her shortly after her diagnosis, a grandmother that was also dying of cancer, and a serial killer that had connections on the outside and was able to torment her family.

Hope. Yeah, there wasn't much of that to go around these days.

"I do need to say one more thing," Emerson said. He shifted a bit and pulled a pamphlet out of the folder he had sitting on his lap. From what Rachel could tell, the pamphlet was the only thing the folder contained. "Speaking of hope…there's this."

He handed the pamphlet to her, and she saw that it was really nothing more than a postcard style piece of marketing. It was simple and minimal, with quite a bit of fine print on the back.

"What's this?"

"This is an experimental treatment that could potentially shrink the tumor. And as it shrinks, its shape also changes. There's some chemotherapy involved, but not in the traditional sense. It's based on a very new and, therefore, experimental use of CAR T-cell therapy. For people beyond a certain age, it's too risky to even recommend, but with you…well, with your age and aside from the tumor itself, you're in pretty amazing physical condition. I think you'd make a suitable candidate for a trial."

"What is it, exactly? And explain it like I'm ten years old, please."

Emerson grinned and took a moment to think of how to do this. "So, we'd use your white blood cells as a tumor-marker of sorts. By labeling them as tumor-specific, those white blood cells viciously attack the tumor. It's sort of like giving your body ballistic missiles to start blasting the tumor with. That, with some minor and very closely-regulated chemo could give you a chance."

"Could?"

"Yes. Your tumor is so far along that even if the approach goes perfectly, the chances of a full cure are small."

"How small?"

"Less than ten percent."

Rachel was ashamed for wanting to hand the little card right back to him. Instead, she clutched it tightly and asked: "How would the treatments affect my physical condition in terms of work?"

He looked surprised for only a moment, maybe even shocked. "It's impossible to know for sure. On days you show up for the treatment, it will likely wipe you out for a day or so. And the chemo rounds for this aren't anything major, but that would progress as needed."

"So in other words...?"

"In other words, there's no way to know for sure."

Rachel nodded, still holding the information he'd given her, and got to her feet. "Thanks, doctor. I appreciate it."

"Mrs. Gift, ten percent is better than nothing. I wouldn't even bother mentioning something so experimental if I didn't think it might be at least worth trying. In this line of work, yes, I see a lot of this sort of thing fail. But here and there, when I least expect it, I see the miraculous, too."

She reached the door and looked back at him, not sure how to respond. She tucked the card into her back pocket and shrugged. "Thanks. But I haven't been feeling anything close to miraculous as of late."

She opened the door and started walking through it. Emerson called out once more, causing her to pause.

"Just think it over. You're healthy enough where it may just be worth a shot."

Rachel gave a quick nod and then left Dr. Emerson in the room alone. She made her way out to reception, settled up her insurance and payment, and then made her way out to the parking lot.

Just think it over. You're healthy enough where it may just be worth a shot.

It was an encouraging comment and the idea of having at least some shred of hope in terms of beating this thing was appealing. The smaller amount of chemo was also appealing. The misery she'd heard from so many chemotherapy stories was one of the initial reasons she'd decided she wasn't going to seek any treatment. But now, with this very small chance, it felt a little different.

Maybe she *should* see what she could do. Maybe she should—

Her phone rang, yanking her out of her wondering. It was just after lunch and now that Peter had all but turned his back on her (he hadn't called or texted in about four days) any call during the midday was likely to be from work. But she'd requested the day off for the appointment, for the expected recovery from the news of the appointment, and to take Paige to dinner and ice cream.

Worried that it was Director Anderson or her partner, Jack Rivers, she dug the phone out of her pocket. She was surprised when she saw

Grandma Tate on the display screen. Getting a call from her while coming out of an appointment for her own mostly secret cancer felt a little eerie—almost like she knew something.

She answered the call as she got into her car. Her heart seemed to slow for a moment, worried that Grandma Tate was calling with bad news—that a recent doctor's appointment revealed she no longer had a year or so, but just a few weeks.

"Hey, Grandma," she answered. "How are you?"

"I'm fine. Well…that may not be totally true. I'm *here*. So I suppose that's something. But look…I did have something to ask you."

Now more worried than ever, Rachel gripped the phone tighter. "Sure. What is it?"

"Do you have a spare key?"

The question baffled Rachel at first and she wasn't quite sure how to respond. "Spare key? What do you…what?"

"A spare key. I'm parked outside of your house and there's no one home. And I'd really like to go in and use the bathroom."

"You're at my house?"

"Yes."

"Your drove there today? To my house?"

"Yes, dear. And I have to use the bathroom. So if you don't mind…"

"There's no key. But you can punch the code into the electric lock. It's 1-9-5-5."

"Oh, that's handy. Thanks."

"Is everything okay, Grandma Tate?"

"I'm not sure. I think we need to talk about some things. But first…I really need your toilet. When will you be home?"

"In actually have the day off. I can be there in about twenty minutes."

"Perfect. I'll see you then."

"Well, what is—"

But her grandmother hung up, ending the call. With her mind racing with what Grandma Tate might have to talk to her about face-to-face, Rachel cranked the car and hurried home. She was thinking about last wills and testaments, about her grandmother preparing for her final days. And all of a sudden, the card Dr. Emerson had given her seemed much more relevant.

CHAPTER THREE

When she arrived home, Rachel found that Grandma Tate had made herself right at home. She'd put on a fresh put of coffee and had scrounged around in the fridge, helping herself to last night's spaghetti and meatball leftovers. She was sitting at the kitchen bar, looking around at the room. Rachel was pretty sure Grandma Tate had not visited for about five years or so. It was one of those trips where it was just so much more enjoyable for everyone to go down and visit her. They'd had new countertops and cabinets put in since then and she was taking it all in.

"Hey, Grandma," Rachel said. She went to her and gave the woman a hug. She felt just how small and frail she was. It was a feeling that was totally in conflict with Grandma Tate's bright and shining face.

"Hey! I wasn't sure if you'd eaten yet, so I warmed up more for you. It's in the microwave."

Rachel had not eaten yet, so she took the bowl out of the microwave and sat down across from Grandma Tate. She stared at her for a moment, smiling.

"Okay," Rachel said. "Don't get me wrong. I'm very happy you're here. But what made you decide to make an unannounced trip to Richmond?"

"Well, it's like I said on the phone. I have to talk to you about something, and it's not anything I could go over on the phone."

"Are you…well, are you okay?"

Taking one more bite of her lunch, Grandma Tate reached over to the edge of the bar where her she had set her purse. She reached inside and pulled out an envelope. She handed it to Rachel—a gesture that was a bit too similar to Dr. Emerson handing her the informational card just half an hour ago.

"I received this in the mail four days ago," Grandma Tate said. "I almost called you right away but decided not to because I thought it might be some sort of cruel prank. I'm rather glad I waited because I did some thinking on it over the last few days and…well…just have a look."

Rachel studied the envelope before looking inside. It had been mailed, the stamp in the upper right corner and the blue post-mark stamp for delivery as well. The envelope had already been opened, and she was able to easily pull the single sheet of folded paper out. She unfolded it and read the very brief note.

Sorry to hear you're not going to make it much longer. At least you won't go alone. Did you know RACHEL is going to be just as DEAD as you very soon?

—   Age
nt   Rachel
Gift's   NO.1
FAN!!!

Fear and anger collided in her heart. She felt both sick and enraged, wanting to throw up and wanting to break something all at the same time It was nearly dizzying.

"This was in your mailbox?" Rachel asked.

"Yes."

"You should have called me right away."

"Why? What would you have done? And I know you've been having some…well, some issues as of late."

"What issues?" She said it fast, nearly snapping at her. What did she know? Rachel knew that she'd revealed she and Peter were having some problems, but Grandma Tate had no idea that he had pretty much left her. And she'd kept every single bit of her tumor diagnosis away from her.

"I've been around, sweetie. I know a thing or two. You've been stressed both times I've seen you lately, and I think it has more to do with my being sick than you've wanted to tell me."

"Things have been…difficult, sure."

"Rachel, is there any truth to this letter?"

"I really don't think so. But if you've received this, it means…well, it means that I have to let my direct supervisor know."

"Why? Rachel, what's happened?"

She started slowly as she walked her grandmother through the events that had transpired with Alex Lynch. The dead squirrel in Paige's room, his threatening phone calls to her, all of it. When she was done, she stared at the envelope and felt tears of anger stinging her eyes. "I don't know how he got your address."

"Well, at least it was mailed. It's not like he came to my house and dropped it at my door."

The thought of this terrified Rachel and she had to look away from her grandmother and the letter for a moment, not wanting to start crying in front of her.

"One more question," Grandma Tate said. "What does he mean about you being dead?"

A very easy lie was on her tongue, ready to be spoken. It would have been so easy. Alex Lynch was only trying scare them, making them think that he could send someone to kill Rachel. It was a simple, believable lie. But with her grandmother *right there*, having driven all the way to see her based on this letter. Besides...Peter knew, and now Jack knew. Her diagnosis wasn't exactly a secret anymore.

When the tears threatened to fall this time, she let them. She didn't even bother wiping them away.

"Rachel?"

"The timing is...sort of cosmic. It seems like you and I might be dying together."

"What? Rachel, what the hell are you talking about?"

She took a deep breath, doing what she could to keep her emotions in check. "About two months ago, I blacked out at work. It came with little blind spots, white specks in my vision. Terrible headaches. I got it checked out and found out there's a tumor on my brain, sort of woven into it and pressing down. It's situated where surgery is impossible without killing me."

Her grandmother's face scrunched up and her eyes glimmered with tears. She reached out with a trembling hand and took Rachel's. "Why...why didn't you tell me?"

"Because you were dealing with your own bad news. You were—"

"How long do you have?"

"A year. Maybe sixteen months at most."

Grandma Tate got down from her stool at the bar and wrapped her arms around Rachel. They wept together for several minutes, a void of time in which Rachel momentarily lost herself to the grief. It was the first time she'd wept tears of total sorrow since getting the news and it felt good in a way that she had not expected. She lost track of time, losing herself to it.

When they finally pulled apart, Rachel saw a heaviness on her grandmother that told her there was more to come. More questions, more hardship to face.

"This man—this Alex Lynch. He knows?"

"He seemed to just sense it in me. He knew without me telling him."

"How's that even possible?"

"I don't know. It was..." She didn't know how to finish the sentence, but the shudder that passed through her seemed like a fitting bit of punctuation. "And while I'm just exposing my stupid soul to you, I may as well tell you that Peter's gone."

"Gone?"

"He left. He got mad about the Alex Lynch thing and was mad because I kept the diagnosis from him for so long. He couldn't handle it and he's gone."

"What an asshole."

The bubble of laughter that erupted from Rachel was genuine and unexpected. She clasped her hand over her mouth, not liking the way her laughter sounded right on the heels of a bout of gut-wrenching weeping.

"Well, he sort of is. I mean...to leave you when...oh, God. Rachel, have you told Paige?"

"No. She's just now finally processing your bad news. I haven't been able to tell her. She's had to deal with the Lynch nonsense in her room, then your bad news, and I just couldn't bring myself to tell her."

"You know you have to, right?"

"I know."

"Today. When she gets home from school. We'll take her out for ice cream, and we'll tell her."

"I don't know if I can."

"You have to. She has to know. You have to get everything in order."

Rachel tried her best to give Grandma Tate a smile as she said, "Now you're sort of being an asshole."

"Oh, I know. And I'm pretty great at it."

There was shared laughter between them at this and while it was genuine, Rachel felt that that it was thin and temporary. After all, they'd both been given grim news of a very similar nature and from here on out the only thing that would truly link them, aside from their love for one another, was quickly looming death.

And in a defiant sort of way, Rachel would much rather face that death head-on than have to break the news to her daughter.

CHAPTER FOUR

As was the case for most children under the age of ten that Rachel had ever met, the highlight of dinner and ice cream was the ice cream. This was a rule that held firm and true for Paige Gift when Rachel and Grandma Tate took her out for burgers and ice cream. They had burgers at Paige's favorite fast-food spot—burgers she'd always loved but Rachel found dry and flavorless—and then sundaes at Scoops and Smiles.

They had their ice cream outside of the shop, on a picnic table. A gentle summer sun seemed to whisper about fall showing up in a few weeks. It was an afternoon that warmed Rachel's heart but was also tainted by the heaviness of what she was about to tell her daughter. And even before she could bring herself to tell Paige about her diagnosis, she was plagued by her own thoughts of what her daughter's life was going to look like.

At some point, she and Peter were going to have to sit down and talk. They needed to figure out what the next few months were going to look like. They needed to get on the same page for how to coach a young girl through the loss of a mother. And somehow, she and Peter were going to need to mend their fences as well as they could. For Paige to come through this ordeal, they were going to have to have their shit together. It was a train of thought that made her not want to tell Paige. Not yet. Not with Grandma Tate here. Jesus, wasn't that like some really messed up double-whammy, to tell your daughter that you were dying while your already-dying grandmother sat across the table, too?

But maybe it would be easier with Grandma Tate here. Any kind of support would be welcome, and Paige had always truly cherished just about anything her great grandmother had ever told her.

"How's the sundae?" Grandma Tate asked Paige.

"So *gooood.*" To show her enthusiasm, she delivered another massive spoonful of her peanut butter cookie dough sundae into her mouth. Then, through a mouthful of squishy goodness, Paige asked: "You just got vanilla?"

"Yes. Can't go wrong with vanilla."

Rachel took another spoonful of her butterscotch, smiling at the pair and trying to summon the courage to bring up her condition with Paige. She was a strong girl and would handle it okay, she supposed. There would be some confusion and tears but by the time their ice cream was eaten (or mostly melted in the paper cups), she'd have unburdened herself of keeping this secret form her daughter and she could move on to the next step. What that step was, she wasn't quite sure, but she supposed it would be revealed to her.

"Hey, why couldn't Daddy come?" Paige asked. "He *never* misses out on ice cream!"

It was a question Rachel had hoped would not come up. She'd just barely skirted over the current set-up with Peter when she and Grandma Tate had spoken earlier.

"I told you, sweetie, he's just got to work really late for the next few weeks. It's one of the reasons Grandma Tate has come to visit."

Paige nodded, satisfied with the answer. Grandma Tate's face tightened as she bit back a disappointed expression. Apparently, she did not approve of the lie, as innocent as it may be.

"How long are you staying, Grandma?" Paige asked. A little trail of dark, melted ice cream ran down her chin as she spoke. She just barely caught it with her napkin and then smiled to her mother and grandmother in embarrassment.

"Oh, maybe just a day or two. Your grandma doesn't usually do things spur of the moment, so this is new for me. How long would you like for me to stay?"

"Like a month?"

"Oh, I don't think I should stay that long." She glanced up to Rachel, her eyes inquisitive and searching. They seemed to say: *What are you waiting for? The ice cream isn't going to last much longer...*

She'd been forced to tell Peter because of Alex Lynch's interference in their lives. And Jack only found out because she'd used her own experience to distract an armed suspect. But here, with her daughter, it was going to have to come naturally. It was going to be an actual discussion.

And Rachel hated that something just felt wrong about it. She tried her best to tell herself that she wasn't just making excuses but there was a certain sort of energy to the moment, a sort of sense of detachment that made her feel this was not the time or the place. Maybe tonight at bedtime, when Paige was in the familiar surroundings of her bed, or maybe at—

When her phone rang in her pocket, it scared her to the point of letting out a small, strangled cry. The timing had just been awful and when she reached to pull it out, her cheeks flushed red with embarrassment.

Both Paige and Grandma Tate had a good laugh over this, which made Rachel feel a little less bad about taking the call. Especially when she recognized the number as coming from one of Director Anderson's offices.

She turned slightly away from the table as she took the call. "This is Agent Gift."

"Gift, I know you asked for the day off, and I've technically given that to you," Director Anderson said from the other end of the line. "But there's a case I need you and Rivers to take tomorrow. You'll be flying to New Mexico, and I'd like for you to come in tonight in order to get briefed on it. I really do hate to step on your toes with this, but you two are perfect for it. And I think it's one you're going to want, anyway."

"When do we fly out?"

"You'd be booked on a red-eye at two o'clock tomorrow morning." He hesitated for a moment, perhaps waiting for Rachel to comment or ask questions. "Are you...well, was your appointment today okay? Are you able to do this?"

"Yes, of course." The answer was out of her mouth before she really even thought about it. The guilt came rushing forward right away. Not only would she be leaving Paige again, but she'd have to politely ask Grandma Tate to either leave this evening (which, with a six-hour drive, she had no intention of doing) or ask her to stay to keep Paige.

But deep down, she was relieved to now have a logical excuse to delay this talk with Paige. "When do you want us in for briefing?"

"Ten o'clock tonight. Can you do that?"

"Yes, sir."

They ended the call and Rachel could feel Grandma Tate's eyes on her before she even looked over in her direction. When she finally did meet her gaze, her grandmother didn't look quite as upset as Rachel had expected. Rachel supposed that, because they were sharing the same fate, her grandmother understood some of the hesitancy and fear she felt when it came to trying to come clean about her diagnosis—especially to Paige.

"Work?" Grandma Tate asked.

"Yeah." She scooped some of her ice cream up into her mouth, considering. But even before she could think of a way to approach what needed to come next, Grandma Tate beat her to it.

"How long do I need to stay?" she asked.

"It would be a few days." Paige looked to her now, apparently picking up on the conversation. "They need me to go to New Mexico."

"When?"

"I leave on a red-eye at two in the morning. But I couldn't ask you to stay and watch her. I mean, with what you've got going on…"

"Nonsense. I feel perfectly fine. Maybe a little tired here and there."

"Wait," Paige said. "You mean Grandma Tate could actually watch me while you're gone?"

"See, Paige thinks it's a wonderful idea!"

"Well, we can take a look at Paige's choice of ice cream flavors and tell that she doesn't always know what she's talking about."

"Hey!" Paige said, holding her spoon out accusingly at her mother.

"Rachel, I'd be honored. And it'll be fun."

She thought about it for a moment. If Grandma Tate had not gotten her own heartbreaking diagnosis, it would be a no-brainer. But she also had no idea how her grandmother's cancer was affecting her on a day-to-day basis. She eyed her across the table, holding her gaze.

"Level with me. Would you be able to do it?"

"Listen to me: the diagnosis itself has been the worst part yet. There's no real discomfort and I've been able to live how I want, for the most part. But at the risk of sounding morbid, it'll only be that way for another several months. So maybe I *should* do this now…while I can."

It was a good point and hard to argue. "Fine. You can watch Paige."

"Yay!" Paige said, clapping her hands with a mouthful of ice cream.

As Paige was wrapped up in her moment of triumph, Rachel leaned closer to her grandmother. "I'm going to call my usual sitter and let her know. If you need *anything,* you call her right away. Can we agree to that?"

"Absolutely. That's fair. But in return, I just ask that you finally have that conversation with your daughter when you get back."

Rachel couldn't bring herself to verbally agree to it, so she just nodded. And even that felt a bit too much like a commitment.

***

15

With a little girl to tuck into bed and a grandmother to update on house rules and family policies, Rachel didn't get any time for a nap before having to leave the house for the ten o'clock briefing at Anderson's office. Before heading out, Grandma Tate reassured her that they would be perfectly fine. It helped ease Rachel's mind a bit, but not as much as the phone call she made to their usual sitter, where she explained the situation and got confirmation that she had a back-up plan if it came to that.

It was a lot to process as she entered the field office just shy of ten o'clock. She entered through the quiet lobby and took the elevator up to the second floor. When she reached Anderson's office, the door between the small waiting room and his office was open since his assistant worked a basic nine-to-five shift. She was not surprised to see Jack already there, sitting on the front side of Anderson's desk. Without a wife or kids to attend to, he was usually the first to these sorts of meetings—something of a running, good-natured joke the two shared.

"Right on time," Anderson said, nodding to the seat beside Jack. "Please, have a seat."

"And how early were you?" she asked Jack as she settled in.

"Been here since seven. Pretty much solved the whole thing without you."

"All jokes aside," Anderson said, giving them both a look of vague warning, "we don't have a whole lot of information on this." He passed a single folder across the desk, which Rachel grabbed and opened up.

She was accustomed to seeing dead bodies and blood in the photos kept in file folders but the first glimpse of a body from a new case was always a little jarring—especially when it was of the sort of graphic nature as the one that sat in front of all of the other case material. There were several photos, which she divided between herself and Jack.

All seven of the pictures showed a woman splayed out on a large, sand-colored rock. The women were nude and splattered with blood. The blood seemed to have come from slits in their necks and their chests torn open. Some of the other photos showed what appeared to be intentional, circular spots of blood by each hand. The photos showed two different women, from two different scenes. They both looked relatively young.

"This is New Mexico?" Jack asked.

"Yes. And given the posed posture and the very exposed nature of the sites, the local PD down there is assuming it's ritualistic. Gift, I thought of you for this one because I know you were gunning for this sort of thing earlier in your career. There's an agent out of Albuquerque that's already on it but is requesting help."

"Is he in agreement that the murders are ritualistic, too?"

"Yes. As you'll see in the notes, there's enough circulating rumors of cult activity out near the Chihuahua Desert to point in that direction. As is the contact information for the agent and the local PD contacts."

"My God," Jack said, cringing at the pictures. "The hearts have been removed?"

"Right again," Anderson said. "So, you can see why they're requesting more help. It's going to get on the news sooner rather than later and it would be nice to already have the case closed before the public gets a chance to panic."

Rachel had always assumed there was a morbid side to her brain because whenever she saw photos and heard details like these, she instantly wanted the case. It was more than just finding justice for these two women, but also the very nature of the case itself. It felt different and challenging. She still felt that way as she leafed through the report, but there was also the fact that she was leaving her recently-cancer stricken grandmother to care for her daughter. And lurking behind all of that was the fact that her own ailments had caught up to her in some form or another during at least one point in each of the last two cases she'd taken.

But looking back to the photos, she knew she'd be unable to turn it down. Also, Anderson was right; during the first two years of her career, she had pushed hard for any cases involving ritualistic symbolism or the occult. She'd eventually been steered elsewhere because of her knack for getting into the minds of serial killers, of understanding what makes them tick and how to apprehend them.

"As you both know, the FBI is no longer labeling fringe groups as *cults.* But it's something we have to consider. There are a few of those groups out that way, most notably The Five Fathers and the Lord of Righteousness Church. Neither of those have ever been suspected of murder of any sort, but there are off-shoots of those two and several others that are being looked into as we speak."

Looking through the notes with Jack leaning over to get a better look as well, Rachel tapped the paper she was currently looking at. "It says both bodies were discovered at least three miles away from any major roadway."

"Exactly," Anderson said. "It's just one of the many reasons the bureau offices out there are requesting our help."

Rachel closed the folder and looked to Jack. He shrugged and clapped his hands together in a matter-of-fact *are we done here* sort of way.

"Anything else, sir?" Rachel asked.

"No. Just to try to get some sleep on the flight. Red-eye flights are a bitch, and that desert heat is going to sap the energy right out of you."

"Thanks for the encouragement, sir," Jack said as he and Rachel made their way toward the door.

When they were back out in the hallway and heading for the elevator, Jack wasted no time expressing his concern—a concern Rachel had been expecting but was truly hoping would remain quiet. As he reached out and pushed the button for the elevator, he asked: "You going to be okay with this?"

"Yes, Jack."

"Hey, just asking. As a friend *and* a partner that you're about to spend a few days with."

"I know. But keep in mind, I've been dealing with this for over six weeks now and so far, I managed to keep it from you."

"Oh, I know," he said as they stepped on the elevator. "And that's the part that has me worried."

CHAPTER FIVE

Rachel did manage to grab a bit of sleep on the plane. She started to doze shortly after take-off but was stirred awake by some turbulence over Missouri. When she opened her eyes, she found Jack flipping through the in-flight magazine. She grinned sleepily; looking through the in-flight magazine was a very Jack thing to do.

"You've got to be the only person that reads that, you know?"

"Maybe," he said, not bothering to look over at her. "But we'll see who's laughing when you need to know the five key hot spots for dining in the Maldives."

She rolled her eyes at him and reached into the netting along the back of the seat in front of her, where she always kept her phone. During the drive from the field office to the airport, they'd been sent digital copies of the files and she'd downloaded them for ease of access on the plane. It was something she'd made a habit of doing so she never found herself empty-handed when they needed vital information in a hurry.

"So, before you get into that," Jack said, "I'd like permission to ask you just one more question about your situation."

"Situation?"

"The cancer. The tumor."

"I knew what you meant," she said with a sly smile. "But honestly, the term *your situation* somehow sounds worse than either *cancer* or *tumor*. Now, what is it you'd like to know?"

"Did you go see Dr. Emerson?"

She really didn't want to go too deep into the weeds on talk of her diagnosis, but she felt she owed Jack at least that much. He had, after all, recommended Emerson. And in their line of work, they had to have each other's back. With the big secret out in the open in front of them, what was the harm in providing extra details?

"Yes. I saw him. I actually had a follow up with him today. Well, at this point, I guess it was yesterday."

"Anything promising?"

"Not at first glance. He says there's this very experimental program that he thinks I'd be a good candidate for. There's a very small chance that it would work, but it's something, at least."

"Are you going to give it a try?"

"I don't know yet."

"Well, can you—"

"I thought you said you only had one question," she interrupted.

"Yeah, but these are follow-ups."

She was slightly disarmed at the fact that he seemed to have brightened a bit when she mentioned the experimental approach. The last thing she wanted to do was offer anyone a form of hope that would only exist to be destroyed about ten or twelve months down the road. She knew it was irrational, but she felt a little irritated at his glimmer of positivity.

To take her mind off of it, she turned her attention back to her phone and pulled up the case files. She read the details and committed them to memory, trying to get a feel for the victims and the sort of man that may have carried the acts out.

Two women: Malorie Osborne, twenty-four years old, and Valerie Mitcham, twenty-two. Malorie had been from Albuquerque while Valerie was from a little town called Foxham. Both women had been killed in the same way—their throats slit, with their chests cut open. They'd then been placed nude and with their arms and legs outstretched on large rocks out in the middle of the Chihuahua desert. So far, no connections had been made between the victims and there were no leads at all. The bodies had been found in totally different areas of the desert, an estimated twenty-six miles apart. This was easy to imagine, as the Chihuahua desert occupied of a space of nearly one hundred and forty thousand miles.

The chests being cut open and the hearts being removed led her to believe it almost *had* to be some sort of ritual. But she knew not to jump to such a conclusion before they had compiled facts of their own.

She had no idea why, but the most jarring part of the photos for her were the little circular splotches of blood purposefully placed on the rocks by the women's hands. This little detail spoke of something more than intentionality or just displaying the heartless bodies as an act of bragging or symbolism. No, those little marks seemed to speak of something bigger…something darker.

Jack leaned over, and nearly whispering it in her ear, said: "I'm leaning toward cult."

"Any reason?"

"The way the arms were extended made me instantly think of depictions of Christ on the cross. And I wonder if the halos of blood by the hands are supposed to represent the nails in his palms."

"Christianity and cults are sort of two different things, you know."

"Depends on who you ask," he responded with a devilish smile.

"If it's Christian in nature, I'd assume it's some way off-base non-traditional group. But I really don't think it matters anyway because I doubt it's a reference to Christ."

"Okay," he said, enjoying the back and forth. "Explain."

"Traditionally, killers that impose Christian symbols in their acts go all out. There's no guess work. If you wanted to go for Christlike symbology, a rock out in the desert would be the last place you'd put the body."

"Maybe something to do with Moses? Weren't Moses and the Israelites stuck wandering in the desert for like forty years?"

"Look at you with all the Bible knowledge."

Jack shrugged. "Lots of Sunday school as a kid. I only went for the animal crackers, though."

"I think we'll know more once we can actually see the wounds. Attacking the chest like that—removing the heart…seems a little excessive, right?"

"Yeah, I was thinking the same thing. Unless, of course, there's some hidden message to it. And an opened chest cavity, left empty and exposed to the air. Maybe something to do with vulnerability?"

Rachel nodded, continuing to look the notes over. There was enough to form the outline of a picture, but now they needed to color it in. The notes they had were presenting a grisly picture, but she was all but sure there was an easy-to-follow story buried somewhere deep within it. Their job, of course, was to find it and to understand it.

And to bring it to an end before any further chapters could be written.

CHAPTER SIX

They arrived at the airport in Albuquerque just a bit after six a.m., GMT. With no bags to rush to retrieve (they always brought carry-ons) they were able to take their time getting off of the plane. As they stepped off of the airbridge and into the airport, Rachel's mind was admittedly focused on getting a cup of coffee first and foremost. But as she started scanning the concourse for the familiar green and white logo of America's most well-known coffee, she spotted the young woman dressed in a very basic and dark uniform that practically screamed FBI. A thin strip of white showed through under the half-buttoned jacket, her collar of her undershirt slightly popped up around her neck. It all made her light brown hair look even lighter. She was standing by the very border of their gate, watching the passengers step into the airport.

"Well," Jack said softly, "she's not going for subtle, that's for sure."

"And you are?"

Jack looked down guiltily at his very basic bureau threads and shrugged. "You got me there. But when have I ever been subtle?"

The young woman stepped forward and gave them a soft smile. "Agents Gift and Rivers?"

"That's us," Rachel said. "I'm Rachel Gift."

"And I'm Jack Rivers." When he extended his hand for a shake, Rachel watched the new agent's face. Jack was a very good-looking man and she'd seen more than a few potential leads and law-enforcement liaisons get a little swept up in his looks and charm. This woman, though, showed none of that and Rachel silently commended her for it.

"Good to meet you both. My name is Melissa Duvall, special agent out of Albuquerque."

Rachel guessed Duvall to be no older than twenty-five. She was young enough to make Rachel wonder how long she'd been a special agent rather than a new agent trainee. Had they tasked her and Jack with this assignment because of this woman's inexperience, maybe?

"You didn't have to meet us at the airport," Rachel said.

"It's not a big deal. I was thinking we could make it out to the most recent crime scene before the sun starts to do its worst. We can head out to the first one, too, if you like. But it's been upwards of one hundred degrees these last few days and that site is pretty much baked. The blood had dried and was already starting to flake away in some places."

The idea of it was enough to make Rachel feel like she was sweating. She'd been to New Mexico twice before, but neither of those visits had been during the summer. Neither of those visits had consisted of her wandering out into the desert, either, for that matter.

As the trio made their way out of the airport, Rachel noticed that Duvall kept casting glances her way, as if she was being studied. It didn't make her uncomfortable, but she was highly aware of it. Rachel knew that for a period of about two years, her name was being circulated throughout the bureau with an almost folktale status. In one year alone, she'd brought down three serial killers and assisted a team overseas with securing a fourth. It had been a landmark year for her. and she knew that some field offices were still using a few of those captures as case studies for agents in training. She couldn't help but wonder if Melissa Duvall had been in one of those sessions and knew a great deal about her career.

"How far away is the site?" Jack asked.

"About fifty minutes away," Duvall said. "The scenery really isn't much and makes it seem a bit longer, if I'm being honest."

They reached Duvall's car in a secondary parking garage and were on the road less than twenty minutes after getting off the plane. Rachel liked the feeling of moving forward, of a case that had wheels to it.

"I assume you've read all the reports?" Duvall asked.

"We have," Rachel said. She was sitting in the passenger seat while Jack, ever the gentleman, had elected to take the back seat.

"We were discussing it on the plane," Jack said. "What do you think of the possibility that it might be related to some sort of religious symbolism?"

"You mean the Christ-like imagery with the arms outstretched?" Duvall said. "Probably not. People going for that sort of symbolism don't mess around. The scene and setting just don't seem right."

Rachel turned her head and gave Jack an *I told you* look. He rolled his eyes and looked out of the rear passenger window as the desert started to glow with the first true morning light.

Rachel looked over to Duvall and studied her fixed, concentrated look as she drove them deeper into the desert. There was a very thin grin on her face, an indication that she was enjoying the company, or just the drive itself. Rachel thought it might be a bit of both.

"Do you get a lot of this sort of thing out here?"

"Ritual-style murders, you mean?"

"No. Just murders that start piling up out in the desert."

She thought about it for a moment before giving a little shrug. "Stragglers here and there, sure. And Lord knows there's probably countless bodies out there that no one knows about or will ever find. It sounds morbid, but we have more than enough proof that any undiscovered body would be nothing but bones within three to four days because of desert critters and vultures. And this time of year, the heat doesn't help at all, either.

"But I'm rambling. Sorry. No…there have never been any mass abundance of cases out this way. Now if you cross the border into Mexico and look into some of the stuff that goes down on the Mexican Plateau, then that's a different story. Drug deals gone bad, prostitutes killed and discarded, missing children showing up dead in the desert about two months after their disappearance. Some really vile shit. We've never seen any of it cross over, though."

Jack made a little whistling noise from the back seat as he looked out to the sunbaked desert, the oranges, reds, flat yellows, and a world of tans and burnt umber. "God, it must feel like you're on another planet out there. I'd be terrified to venture too far out into all of that."

"Too bad for you," Duvall said with just a bit of sarcasm. "Because you're going to be walking through a pretty good chunk of it in about half an hour."

***

Duvall drove her little sedan as far down the small desert road as she could. She'd turned off the main road nearly ten minutes ago, finally bringing her car to a stop in a mostly flat area that was slightly discolored from the surrounding area. Several old wooden posts stuck up roughly three feet in the air, creating a rectangle. Cross ties ran between them on the ground, creating a little parking area of sorts.

As they got out of the car, Rachel was surprised to find just how cool the morning was. It was extremely pleasant—maybe even just a tad bit chilly.

"So, we're walking straight ahead for about a mile," Duvall said. "After that, there are a few different public trails that wind up into the hillier regions about six miles to the west. But we're skipping all of that and taking a more direct route—the route we're pretty confident the killer took."

"We?" Jack asked. "Where *is* the local PD this morning?"

"I asked them to stay behind. They're understandably panicked. I didn't want too many bodies out here while you guys got your first glimpse. But as soon as we get out of here and into the town of Foxham, they're ready to help however needed."

"Foxham," Rachel said as they started walking, passing by the wooden posts. "That's where the second victim was from, right? Valerie Mitcham?"

"That's right. They're working in tandem with the State PD out of Albuquerque. They all seemed to be perfectly fine being hands off for as long as we needed. Of course, we also have full FBI resources out of my field office."

"Our director seems to think we've been asked out her because everyone would like it wrapped up before the news starts reporting it, right?"

"Oh, absolutely. But the first murder has already been on the news. They didn't report all of the grisly details, though. Nothing about heart extraction or the body being fully naked. But when word of this second one gets out, I think the hand has been dealt, you know? And Lord help us if there's a third one."

That comment hung in the air for the next quarter of a mile or so. After that, the staccato sounding crunch of their footsteps on the dry desert floor started to unnerve Rachel. "How long have you been a special agent, Duvall?"

"This is my second year. And, interestingly enough, already my third case that looks to be ritualistic in nature." She chuckled and added, "It's okay. I get it a lot. I know I look young. But I'm twenty-seven, I swear it."

"Some would say that *is* young," Jack commented.

"Did the other two cases turn out to be ritualistic?" Rachel asked.

"One did. It was this weird thing out of Roswell that somehow made it all the way out here. This guy's family had somehow brainwashed him into thinking his family had come here on one of the spaceships that supposedly crashed at Roswell in 1947. When people started laughing at him, he abducted them from their homes, killed them, and then set their bodies in a line out in the desert as offerings to alien beings he believed to be his ancestors. He killed four people in less than eighteen hours."

Looking out to the wide-open spaces all around them, interrupted only by rocks and small brush outcroppings, Rachel found the story all too easy to imagine.

They came to the split where the public pathways slowed up much faster than Rachel expected. Yet almost right away, the terrain started to get rockier and much more unstable. It was more of a workout on the ankles and calves rather than the knees. The heat wasn't getting to her yet (the temperature was still surprisingly comfortable, actually) and if she didn't know they were about to visit the site of a murder, she might have considered it an enjoyable walk.

"One thing is for certain," she said as the ground started to rise a bit more. "The killer has to be in good shape. To lug a body all the way out here would have taken not only crazy determination, but a good deal of strength, too."

"Agreed," Duvall said. "And we're pretty sure he carried them threshold style the entire way. We've combed over the most direct routes numerous times for any signs that the bodies may have been dragged, and there are none. Of course, out here in the desert, there's a limitless number of angles he could approached the rock from."

Rachel was surprised to see just how quickly the ground was flattening out. As it came to an even keel, it then slightly dipped, giving way to an expansive valley. Way out in the distance, a series of mesas and buttes could be seen. But before Rachel could truly start to appreciate the beauty of the sight, Duvall walked a few yards out ahead of them and looked down to the ground.

She was pointing to a large yet short rock formation. It came out of the ground at a slight angle and became more of a formation off to the left where it merged with an outcropping of rock that ran along the side of a hill that wound its way over toward a mountain range.

"This is the rock where Valerie Mitcham's body was found. She was spotted by a pair of hikers from a trail heading up to an overlook partway to Little Squaretop." She then pointed to the left, to the rising ground that curved over toward a more sharply inclined rock formation that sank into the side of the mountains about two hundred yards further out.

Rachel took a look around at the vast space, the limitless possibilities for answers. "What if he didn't carry them? What if he lured them? Or if they were already here themselves?"

"We've looked into those possibilities, too," Duvall said. "But we can find no cars that are unaccounted for in any of the surrounding parking lots. Nothing like that within a range of thirty miles."

"Let me venture back into the cult theory," Jack said. "What if these women were willing to do this? What if they signed up for it and allowed it to happen?"

"You mean what if they were part of a cult?" Duvall asked. "Not likely. Malorie Osborne was an executive vice president of a tech upstart, something to do with NFTs. Looking into her past, we found that she was already earning something of a positive reputation and had made more than two hundred grand in the past seven or eight weeks.

"As for Valerie Mitcham, she was working as an intern for a paralegal company. She was just a few months away from graduating law school. No red flags for either of them. If they were cult members, they hid it well from the people they knew the best."

"Any within a cult or even most fringe groups don't go to such great lengths to hide their affiliations," Rachel pointed out.

She walked to the edge of the rock and peered directly up. There was nothing overhead except a perfect blue sky. The mountains were to the left, the open desert to all other sides. It was odd, but the vastness of the desert seemed to speak of both adventure and death all at once. She seemed strangely in tune with it and couldn't help but wonder if it had something to do with her own approaching death—with the tumor currently pressing into her brain, reaching its tendrils deeper in.

"Have you looked into star maps over the past week or so?" she asked.

"Star maps?" Duvall was clearly confused.

"To see the position of the stars when the bodies were placed out here in the desert. If it *is* cult related and the bodies are being placed in these wide-open spaces, it might be worth looking into. Maybe something to do with planetary alignments or constellations." She realized both Duvall and Jack were looking at her curiously and gave them a shrug. "Probably nothing. Just something to look into."

"Yeah, maybe so," Duvall said. She instantly took her cell phone out and started jotting down the note.

As they fanned out and started looking the area over, Rachel again found herself drawn to the feeling of ever-reaching, empty spaces. The idea of being so free and unbound while also feeling pinned down had her feeling odd. And somewhere deep down, she wondered if that had something to do with why the killer chose this location.

She thought of the hearts of those two women being removed, their bodies splayed on large rocks, and was almost certain the location was a big part of the answers they were looking for. Of course, in this case, the question needed to be discovered first. And so far, all they had was the most basic question of all.

Why?

She wondered if a visit to the coroner's office might point them in the right direction.

CHAPTER SEVEN

One thing Rachel was really starting to like about Duvall was that she was making sure to give her and Jack enough freedom to conduct the case in their own way, but she was also very succinct and to the point. As soon as Rachel mentioned the coroner's office, Duvall agreed completely and led them back to her car without argument or even much discussion. It was clear that she was anxious to get the new agents caught up on everything so she could dive right back into the thick of the case.

Rachel not only respected her for this, but she found herself slightly envious. Here was a girl nearly a decade younger than she was, with her whole career ahead of her. Her whole *life* ahead of her. And she wasn't hindered by a life-ending diagnosis or the need to tell a daughter Mommy was going to die. No, she was a new agent not too long out of training, and she had the world waiting for her right in front of her feet.

As they made their way into town, she began to understand why there were so many dramatic and romantic notions about driving out west, to drive through the American desert. It was awe-inspiring and inviting in a way that other areas of America simply couldn't match. They drove in what appeared to be a straight direction for about nine miles before Duvall turned off onto a stretch of blacktop that was much more faded than the two-lane road. There were also no real markings of any kind. About a mile after the turn-off, they passed a sad-looking road sign that served as an introduction with one simple word: FOXHAM.

Rachel glanced ahead and saw the beginnings of a small town. Slowly, a few more businesses popped up, and then the entrance to a small subdivision. Soon, sidewalks introduced themselves and the road began to show signs of lines down the center.

"How many people live in Foxham?" Rachel asked from the back.

"Just a little over three thousand. And that's a recent number. As recently as seven years ago, it was closer to one thousand. But then the subdivision sprouted up and property values became a little more attractive."

"Still seems a little small to even warrant a coroner's office," Jack remarked.

"Well, it's an interesting set-up. The coroner's office is in the same building as the police department, just downstairs. It's sort of an unofficial coroner's office—for cases that need immediate attention before the bodies are shipped off to Albuquerque. Cases like this one, actually. Now, Malorie Osborne has been moved to Albequerque already. But I asked them to hold Valerie Mitcham's body here when I knew you guys were coming. Figured it made the most sense because it's closer to the murder site."

"Good thinking," Jack said. He was smiling as he looked at her, showing that he was just as impressed with Duvall as Rachel was.

The police station was a small brick building that stood out like blood against the tans and oranges of the desert backdrop. Melissa Duvall parked her car at the side of the building, ignoring the front lot altogether. She then led them into the station from a side entrance that opened up into a brightly lit hallway. Right away, a set of stairs led down into a subfloor. Duvall led them down the stairs and into another hall that was much dimmer and somehow crisper. Had she been blindfolded and then led here to have the blindfold removed, Rachel might have thought she was in a hospital hallway rather than inside a police station.

"The coroner's office is down here, all the way down the hall," Duvall explained. "It's almost like they wanted to keep it as far away from the police as they could, I think."

The hallway was short and occupied by only three rooms. When they came to the end of the hallway, Duvall knocked on the door in front of them and then opened it just a crack. "Shirley? You in here?"

"If that's Duvall, come on in!"

She led Rachel and Jack inside. A large, open room awaited them. It was a typical set-up for an examination room that reminded Rachel more of a morgue than a coroner's office. A single table, shaped like a bed, sat in the middle of the room. A sheet had been tossed over the body that waited beneath. A series of counters wrapped around the back half of the room, adorned with different utensils, trays, and equipment.

A woman that looked to be in her late fifties stood at the back counter, flipping through the pages of a three-ring binder. She turned to greet them, giving them the practiced smile of a woman that had spent her life working jobs where people didn't smile much.

"Agents Gift and Rivers, this is Shirley Baxter—coroner and sometimes ME, depending on the case."

"Pleased to meet you," Shirley said, peering at them from behind a set of stylish eyeglasses. "Agent Duvall told me you'd be coming by, so I already took the liberty of bringing the latest victim out. Valerie Mitcham, age twenty-three. Cause of death...well, that's a pretty obvious one now, isn't it?"

Duvall looked to Shirley as she neared the examination table. "You mind?"

"Help yourself," Shirley said.

Agent Duvall removed the sheet from the top half of the body with a great deal of grace and respect. She was not pulling back the sheet to show off the gross details of a case she was working on; no, she was letting them see a young woman that had been brutally robbed of her life.

As usual, the sight of the real body was a bit more jarring than the photos. Even with the lacerations and opening cleaned and tidied up, it was always somehow worse. In photos, murder victims looked like a living thing that had been killed. On an examination table, Rachel always thought they looked almost like stage design, as if they'd never had life within them at all.

It was a bit different this time, as the opening where the woman's heart had once been was *right there,* proof that a beating heart had once rested inside of it. She and Jack approached the table. Rachel's eyes were pretty much glued to the hole in the woman's chest. In comparison, the gash in her neck seemed somehow trivial. Some of the scars and tears from where carrion birds of the desert had nipped at her were still visible, too, despite having been patched up.

Shirley joined them but gave them their distance. Meanwhile, Duvall stood on the opposite side of the table as if she wanted to make sure she wasn't in the way.

"As you can see," Duvall said, "the slash marks into the flesh and past the tissue are quite even and neat. Likely done with a small, very sharp knife. Maybe even a scalpel of some kind. But then once you get into the finer details, you can see that the killer didn't truly know what he was doing. There are marks and some chipping along the sternum. The cuts to the pericardium look ragged and nasty as opposed to the neat incisions at the skin. Still, the fact that he went under the sternum and left no real portions of the heart behind indicates that he removed it with a great deal of care."

"Is there any way to tell if the heart was removed before or after her throat was slit?" Jack asked.

"Not for sure, but I'd assume the neck came first. Why bother slitting the throat of a woman you've just killed by removing her heart?"

"And what about Malorie Osborne?" Rachel asked. "Was it the same as we see here?"

"To the letter," Shirley said. "I've got the photos after the body was cleaned up if you like."

"I have those, too," Duvall said. "So you'll have access to them."

Rachel nodded, finding it far too hard to take her eyes away from the empty chest cavity. To take a life was one thing. But to take a life by removing the very beating heart that kept the body alive was something different. This killer wanted to prove a point. Even if there was a ritualistic base to his actions, it felt almost personal. And while there was no absolute proof that the killer had taken the heart—it could have been taken by a scavenging desert creature, she supposed—everything about the set-up screamed this was the case.

It started to feel personal to Rachel, too. Because while she'd hoped from the start that continuing to work would distract her from the harsh hand she'd been dealt, this case was doing the exact opposite. She could far too easily see herself on that table, laying under a blanket that she felt served as the meager less than ten percent that Dr. Emerson had given her if she went with the experimental treatment.

Rachel saw herself on the table and felt that even if they caught this killer, that was exactly where she would remain: dead and heartless under a sheet, a hole ripped right into her chest.

Valerie Mitcham's body served as a stark reminder that this fate—*death*—was waiting on her, patiently tapping its foot.

***

Valerie's parents also lived in Foxham, just a quick six-minute drive from the police station, in fact. When they got out of Duvall's car and started up the walk, Rachel could look out to her right and see a sliver of the very same desert in which Valerie had died. She imagined such a thing would be pretty damned hard on grieving parents.

"I was here late yesterday afternoon," Duvall told them as they neared the porch. "Unless something drastic has changed, the mother—Delia Mitcham—is an absolute wreck. She has no idea her daughter's body is still here in Foxham. We had to restrain her from continuously driving to the police station yesterday. It was pretty bad."

As they walked up to the porch and Duvall knocked on the door, Rachel started to feel the first true signs of the day's heat starting to press down on them. Being that it was not even eleven o'clock yet, this did not bode well for the rest of the day.

The door was answered by a grim-looking man. There were crows' feet under his eyes and the corners of his mouth looked to have been recently sculpted by some demented artist so that he would never smile again. His salt-and-pepper hair was in disarray and Rachel could see where it was starting to thin at the temples. There was a brief flash of recognition in his eyes as he saw Agent Duvall.

"Agent Duvall," he said with a stern nod.

"Sorry to bother you again, Mr. Mitcham. But as you can see, I have two more agents with me. I think they're going to be a valuable addition to the team we have on the case. Would you mind if they came in to ask some questions? Many of them may be similar to ones the cops and myself have already asked."

"Sure," he said without much emotion. "But I can tell you right now that Delia won't be joining us. And I'd appreciate it if you wouldn't even approach her. She's been sitting in that parlor of hers since last night and won't come out. She barely even talks to me. Just sits in there and looks at the same three or four pages of a photo album. She screams sometimes, these high-pitched wails, you know?" A tear rolled down the side of his face and he wiped it away quickly. "If she's not doing better by the time the fu..." He stopped here, his breath catching in his throat. He fought with emotion for a while before managing to finish the statement. "If she's not better by the time the funeral comes around, I'm going to have to take her to the hospital." He sighed and then went still for a moment, as if he'd forgotten what he was doing. He blinked the fog away and then stepped aside, letting the three agents enter.

He led them into the house, down a small hallway where a large living room sat on the right. As they made their way, they passed the parlor Mr. Mitcham had mentioned. Rachel quickly glanced inside and saw a woman of Mr. Mitcham's age sitting in an ornate chair with a photo album opened in her lap. She didn't even look up as the three of them passed by. She was very much checked out, staring into some other faraway world in the past.

In the living room, Mr. Mitcham plopped down into an old armchair. He didn't offer for the others to sit, but Duvall did anyway. Rachel followed suit while Jack elected to remain standing. Duvall looked over to Rachel and nodded, giving her and Jack the floor.

"Mr. Duvall, do you know many of Valerie's friends, or maybe even people she only had passing acquaintances with?"

"I know a few of them. She really didn't have all that many to tell you the truth. When she started law school, that became her life. She didn't really have much of a social life. The few close friends she has are at the school—University of New Mexico. She has some friends from high school still living around here, but she sort of dropped them when she started taking school seriously."

"Did you know if she'd had some falling outs with any friends lately?"

"No, none that I know of."

She figured not, but these were the expected warm-up questions. Questions that drew the grieving parents into feeling a sense of comfort. She didn't think for a minute that an estranged friend would drag her out to the desert and then cut her heart out.

"What about the part of the desert she was found in? Did she have any sort of ties to it?"

He laughed a bit and it sounded genuine but also pinched with something close to madness. "No. God no. Valerie hated the desert. She always talked about how pretty it was, but she hated the heat. I'm pretty sure she intended to leave New Mexico when she graduated."

"Do you know where she wanted to go?" Jack asked.

"She always talked about Seattle. She liked the rainy vibe of it, I think."

"I understand she was working as a paralegal, right? An intern?"

"Sort of. She was an intern, yes, but there was some money coming from it, too. Not quite a job but almost. That sort of thing."

"And do you happen to know if she'd been assisting with any controversial cases?"

"Oh, I don't think so."

"I talked to the law firm," Agent Duvall said. "She hadn't been active on any cases. She was more or less helping with research."

Rachel nodded, knowing that her next question had the potential to derail the conversation. But she had to go there. Hopefully, it would go unheard by the already catatonic mother in the parlor.

"Forgive me for asking, but I have to ask: do you know of any sort of odd hobbies or interests Valerie had?"

"Odd how?" He seemed curious, not quite angry or offended yet.

"Anything, really. Maybe astrology, the occult, an interest in serial killers or fringe religions."

Mr. Mitcham still didn't look offended or disgusted. If anything, he looked concerned and actually spent some time thinking about it. "No, not recently. Now, when she was a teenager, she was into some strange music—stuff like Marilyn Manson and some really oppressive, loud music. She was always slightly into horror movies, too, but it was never an unhealthy obsession."

"And what about a boyfriend? Did Valerie have a boyfriend?"

"She did. He's also taken it pretty hard. A nice young man named Jacob Burrow."

"Is he also in Foxham?"

Mr. Mitcham shook his head. "No, he's over in Valens."

Duvall leaned in and, in a soft voice, said, "Another small desert town about halfway between here and Albuquerque."

"Sir, when was the last time you saw her?" Jack asked.

"Five days ago. She came by early and had breakfast with us."

"And did she seem normal that morning? Did you sense anything off or wrong with her?"

"No. Not at all. She was smiling and laughing, in a really good mood. She and her mom were bickering about a few of the clues in the newspaper crossword. She was her usual, perfect self."

His eyes looked away from them, out to the hallway and in the direction of the parlor.

"You'll find who did this, right?"

"We'll do everything we can, sir," Rachel said.

He shook his head as another tear slipped down his face. "The son of a bitch that did this...they took her heart right out of her chest. Agents, do any of you have children?"

Jack and Duvall shook their heads. Rachel took a moment to suppress the chill that rode up her spine before answering. "Yes, sir. I do. A girl. She's eight."

"Imagine some vile person tearing her heart out and leaving her out in the desert for buzzards to peck at."

"Mr. Mitcham, I—"

"You imagine your little girl in that situation, her heart torn out and her life taken from this world, and you tell me if 'We'll do everything we can' is good enough."

Rachel felt like she'd been slapped. And worst of all, her mind did exactly what Mr. Mitcham had suggested. She saw Paige, stripped naked with her heart ripped out of her chest. It made her own heart surge with anger and sorrow. And it was likely why she spoke the words that came out of her mouth—words she, as an agent, was supposed to never utter.

"No, it's not enough," she said, getting to her feet. "You have my word, Mr. Mitcham. We'll find the individual that did this."

With that said, she turned and headed for the door before she had time to feel Jack's alarmed gaze settling on her.

CHAPTER EIGHT

"Rachel, you know you shouldn't have said that."

Jack looked more upset than he sounded. He was sitting shotgun this time while Rachel sat in the back of the car. It was the location she'd chosen when she went outside before Jack and Duvall. For a terrifying moment, she thought she was going to break down in tears, as the image of Paige on that rock out in the desert would not leave her mind. But by the time the two other agents came out of the Mitchams' house, she had it mostly together.

"I know," she said, staring out to the endless canvass of desert to all sides.

"I get it," Duvall said. "That was a pretty harsh move, asking you to picture your daughter like that."

Rachel agreed but didn't want to say it. She didn't want to blame Mr. Mitcham for her moment of unprofessionalism. Wanting to change the subject as quickly as she could, she asked: "How long before we get to the boyfriend's place?"

"Maybe twenty minutes. I went by there shortly after her body was discovered but he'd dipped out to be with his parents for comfort." She hesitated for a moment and then eyed Rachel in the rearview mirror. "Can I ask you something?"

"Sure."

"Do you find the job harder with a kid back home?"

"Yes, most of the time. But she gets it. There are times when she seems very proud that her mommy's job is to help catch bad guys."

"Is there a husband back home to help out?"

Rachel again felt as if she'd been slapped and felt a little twinge of resentment toward Duvall. "That's a little complicated right now. And I'd really rather not discuss it at the moment."

"Oh, of course. Sorry for prying."

"It's not a problem."

The car went quiet, and she noticed Jack trying to check on her in the rearview mirror. But Rachel kept her eyes turned away, once again watching the desert roll by. It did not change at all as they approached the little town of Valens. The desert did not seem to open up and give way to human habitats as easily as the town of Foxham did. For the town of Valens, there was just a thin road that came off of the main road at a harsh right angle. When Duvall turned down the road, Rachel could almost see the entire town. It looked like a little Lego community that had been set up by a well-organized child.

There was a main thoroughfare that shot directly through the center of town, and several offshoot streets that worked in a grid-pattern around numerous buildings. The residential areas sat mostly to the left, in thinner grid-like patterns. She imagined the entire town of Valens looked like nothing more than a very succinct blueprint from an airplane.

Duvall took them just a small way into town, turning left before they were able to see the center of the city. After a few dusty side roads, speckled with cars that glittered in the desert sun, she ventured down a better maintained road that ran alongside a small row of townhomes and an apartment building.

She parked the car in front of the second group of townhomes and the trio once again stepped out into the desert air. Agent Duvall led them up to the third door along the row. She looked back to them as if asking permission to knock and didn't move until Jack gave her a little nod. Apparently, she was starting to feel that the case was now properly shared among them, and she didn't want to come off as if she thought she was running the show. Duvall knocked and stepped back, awaiting an answer.

"It's the middle of the day on a Wednesday," Jack said. "What makes us think he's even home?"

"His girlfriend was brutally murdered," Rachel said. "Unless he's a heartless bastard, I doubt he went in to work."

"Yeah," Duvall said. "He took it *really* hard. They'd just gotten engaged two months ago. Besides," she added, pointing to a blue Honda behind them, "that's Jacob's car."

After another several seconds, there was still no answer. Duvall knocked again. As she did, Rachel stepped over to the only window looking out from along the front of the townhouse. A set of basic white blinds were set up, partially opened. She looked inside for any signs of movement or indicators that the place was empty despite Jacob's car being parked right behind them.

The window looked in on a small, rectangular foyer. Part of her view was blocked off by a wall that gave way to a stairway that led to the second floor. The other half of the view looked in on a tidy open-floor area with a kitchen and living room that were separated by a kitchen bar. On the kitchen-side of the bar, she saw a small two-seater table. A man sat there, a small bottle knocked over on the table. Pills were scattered here and there and—

"Force your way in," Rachel said, stepping back from the window.

"Force my...what?"

"He's about to kill himself."

That was all Jack needed to hear. He tried the knob first and when that did not turn, he took a huge stride back. He came forward in a charge Rachel had seen a few times before. It was a side of him she enjoyed seeing because he let it out so rarely. The man could be a beast if the situation called for it.

It only took the first kick, perfectly aimed just beneath the lock and against the side of the doorframe. Jacob Burrow's door went flying in, the lock base clattering to the floor. Once it was opened, Agent Duvall rushed forward into the kitchen.

The entire ordeal had apparently terrified Jacob. Several pills he'd been cupping in his hand went to the floor. He jumped up from his seat, slamming into the table and sending even more pills to the floor. He raised his hands as if he'd been caught in the middle of committing a heinous crime. Both of them were empty, no pills to be seen.

"How many have you taken, Jacob?" Duvall asked.

"None! I was...scared! I was..."

Rachel eyed the prescription bottle that had toppled over on the table. "Temazepan," she said. "Sleeping pills. Strong ones, too." She also noted the bottle of vodka sitting on the kitchen bar. It looked to have been only recently opened, missing about five or six shots worth.

"Don't bullshit me, Jacob," Duvall said. "How many? I'll count the pills out if I have to."

"None, I swear! I had some vodka, yeah. But when I tried taking the pills, I was too scared." He looked beyond Duvall for the first time, seeing Rachel and Jack. "Do you know something? Did you find who did it?"

"No," Duvall said, backing away from him and sitting down at the table. She started placing the pills back into the bottle, giving Jacob Burrow an irritated look. "That's why we're here. Wanting to talk to you."

"I already talked to you at my parents' house."

"And you weren't in a good place to answer questions."

"Doesn't seem like he is now, either," Rachel said, gesturing to the pill bottle.

Jacob looked around like a lost child and sat down on the floor. He was swaying a bit, perhaps from the five or six shots of straight vodka he'd taken. His feet stretched out in front of him. "It's sad and pathetic, I know. But I can't live without her. I don't *want* to live without her."

His heartbreak seemed genuine, and Rachel found herself hurting for him.

"Can you still not think of anyone that might have done this to her?" Duvall asked.

"No. Not a single person. It doesn't make sense. She liked everyone, and everyone liked her..."

He started weeping, tears streaming down his face. He looked to Rachel and Jack, as if hoping they might be able to offer some sort of solace. Rachel stepped forward and hunkered down to her haunches so that she was closer to eye level with him.

"Jacob, I'm Agent Gift, and this is my partner, Agent Rivers. We're new to the case and anything you could help us with is going to get us to the killer faster. You understand that?"

He only nodded. He then looked to the bottle of vodka, his eyes drinking it in greedily.

"First, I'll ask you the same thing Agent Duvall asked. How many pills did you take?"

"I told you! None."

Rachel looked back to Jack. "Agent Rivers, would you mind counting what Agent Duvall has put back into the bottle?"

Jack took the bottle from the table and uncapped it. As he started shaking them out in his hand, Jacob slammed his hand angrily down on the floor. "Fine! I took six. I took six and then had second thoughts and..."

"Jesus, Jacob," Duvall said. She pulled out her cellphone and Rachel watched as she stepped away, calling 9-1-1.

Rachel knew that six pills was not going to kill him, but when you added in the vodka, it made for a potent cocktail. She still doubted it was a lethal mixture, but she did know that Jacob was going to crash very soon and when he did, he was going to sleep as if he *were* dead. So she was going to have to choose her questions wisely and ask them quickly.

"When was the last time you saw Valerie?"

He winced at the sound of her name, a painful contortion of his face as if he'd been stabbed. "The night it happened. She was here. We had dinner. Made love. Then she left."

"She went home?"

"Yeah."

"Why didn't she stay over?" Jack asked.

"We said we weren't sleeping over anymore. Wanted to save something special for after we were m-m-married."

"Did she seem normal to you that night?" Rachel asked.

"Yeah, same as always. Nothing n-n-new." His breath was hitching now, and Rachel wasn't sure if it was because he was trying not to break down in front of them or if the pills and alcohol were starting to grasp at him.

"Had she been sad or upset at all in the week or so leading up to her death?"

"Not at all. She was getting really excited about all the wedding planning. We'd started arguing about what song we'd d-d-dance to. She...*fuck* this is miserable!"

He slammed at the floor again, this time with both hands. It was like watching a child throw a temper tantrum—only the suicide attempt made it feel much darker than that.

Duvall came back into the room The irritation that had been on her face had morphed into something closer to pity. "An ambulance is on the way."

"What the hell for?" Jacob asked. "I don't want to be here...not without her."

Rachel had never been one for romantic sentiment but the tone in which Jacob said this broke her heart a bit. He wasn't just saying it for romantic effect, but out of genuine pain and loss.

His eyes were glossing over as his punches softened against the floor. Duvall joined Rachel on the floor and snapped her fingers in front of Jacob's eyes. "Jacob, look. We won't ask more questions. I just need you to stay with me for right now, okay? Try your best to stay awake. Just about eight to ten more minutes. Okay?"

"This isn't fair..." he muttered. A little drool bubble formed and popped on his lip as his head slumped. "She's gone. Took her heart and everything. Took her...took..."

"Come on, Jacob, hang in there."

Rachel got to her feet and glanced around the kitchen, looking for any clues. Her eyes immediately went to the refrigerator. There were a few decorative magnets, some of which were little picture holders. There were five pictures in all. Three of them showed Jacob with Valerie Seeing her vibrant and smiling was like looking into the past and it nearly made Rachel dizzy with the context of it all.

Another showed Jacob standing with a younger man, a guy of about eighteen or twenty. The resemblance between the two was uncanny; Rachel assumed it was his brother. But then there was another picture, one that truly caught Rachel's eye. She walked over to it and removed it from the fridge.

There were four people in the picture. Two were Jacob and Valerie. The other two also appeared to be a couple; the woman, a petite red head, had her hand on the chest of the man, hugging him tightly. But the most interesting part of the photo was that it had been taken out in the desert. The four of them appeared to be on a trail by some sort of overlook. Just behind them and slightly below, there was a reddish outcropping of rock. Rachel could tell that it was not the same place Valerie's body had been found, but there were enough similarities to make her stare a bit harder.

"Agent Duvall...any idea who these other two people are?"

Duvall studied the picture and shook her head. She took the photo from Rachel and held it in front of Jacob's hazed-over eyes. "Jacob, I need you to focus." She reached out and actually held his chin in her hands, making him look at her. His eyes fluttered open, and his head swayed.

"Huh..."

"Jacob, who are the other two people in this picture with you and Valerie?"

He blinked furiously, doing his best to answer. He sighed heavily, the breath shuddering as it came out. When he spoke, he sounded like a man that was talking in his sleep—which, Rachel figured, he basically was.

"Kyle and Jill....Browning. They....they're our friends."

His eyes fluttered again and then closed. His head slumped to his chest and right away, his breathing increased. A very deep breath, then a shaky exhale.

"Kyle and Jill Browning," Jack said. "Have those names come up before?"

"No," Duvall said, looking hard at the picture. "Mr. Mitcham said how much Valerie hated the desert, but here she is..."

"They're slightly sweaty and red-faced in the picture," Rachel said. "Maybe they were just out for a hike. Either way, they're the only other people we have to speak with."

"I'll get you their address," Duvall said. "You mind speaking with them on your own? I'm going to ride in the ambulance with Jacob. Maybe he'll come to and offer up something useful."

"Good idea," Jack said. "And if they had friends that they did this sort of stuff with, I wonder if there are more friends that they simply never told their parents about."

"I have a cop looking into their social media. I know Valerie wasn't a big user. She had a Facebook page that hadn't been updated for about seven months and an Instagram page with just two pictures. I should be hearing something soon."

"Sounds like a plan," Rachel said. "We'll meet you at the hospital after we speak with the Brownings."

Taking one look back down to Jacob, Duvall nodded and pulled out her phone. "Let me get you that address."

As she called in the information request with the local PD, Rachel took another look at the picture from the fridge. She focused more on the background than the four people. While it wasn't the spot either body had been found at, it was just far too similar—especially the red colored rock just behind and below them. Because of the details Rachel knew of the cases of Valerie and Malorie, that rock looked like it was waiting for something, as if it knew it might one day be the stage for a brutal act.

CHAPTER NINE

Jack wasn't sure why but splitting up from Duvall made it seem as if the case was really moving along quickly. He usually wasn't a fan of being paired with an unfamiliar agent, but with a case like this, he supposed the more heads put on it, the better. Especially when he was still having a problem feeling safe and confident with Rachel at his side.

To this point, she'd done nothing to make him seriously question her abilities or reasoning, but now that he knew about the tumor, he felt that he was working with a partner that had a ticking bomb strapped to their back. He hated feeling this way but also knew that it was not something he would be able to openly discuss with her. He feared that bringing it up would stress her out even more and cause unnecessary strain between them.

As a federal agent, his chief concern needed to be the case. So long as Rachel was still managing to carry her load, he could save his worries about her for between cases. He also figured that given Rachel's personality, the best way to show his support would be to not mention it unless she brought the topic up first.

Even then, though, the silence in the car as they drove to Kyle and Jill Browning's house was a heavy one. Her tumor was the unspoken issue between them, resting in the car just like a third, unwanted passenger in the back seat. Jack was aware that it was making him slightly uneasy, but he didn't feel he had the right to say anything—to cross that line and bring it up.

By the time he'd started to feel the least bit brave enough to say something, they'd already arrived at the Browning residence. They lived in a charming little house on a lot in an up-and-coming neighborhood just outside of the Albuquerque city limits. When they stepped out of the car and started up the driveway, Jack felt the heat pressing down on them. The gentle temperatures in the desert this morning to the scalding feel of the sun as they approached the Brownings' porch was borderline scary.

Rachel knocked on the door and they shared a quick glance that had become something of a common moment in most instances where they knocked on a door during a weekday. Ten years ago, it would have been considered almost a wasted trip; surely whoever it was they needed to speak to was still at work. However, with the huge increase in work from home jobs, Jack was finding that they usually hit something close to a fifty-fifty rate of people being home during the week.

He mentally marked the Brownings up into that rate when the door was answered roughly twenty seconds after Rachel knocked. The man they'd seen in the picture on Jacob's fridge greeted them. He looked slightly irritated, clearly having been interrupted from something.

"Yeah? Can I help you?"

Jack showed his badge and ID. "Agents Rivers and Gift, FBI. You're Kyle Browning, correct?"

"Yes, that's right. What's this about?" But the sad look in his eyes told Jack that he might already know.

"Are you aware of what happened to Valerie Mitcham?"

Kyle nodded and his shoulders seemed to sag a bit. "Yes. Jacob reached out and told us. It's…well, it's terrible."

"We saw a picture of you and your wife on Jacob's refrigerator," Rachel said. "Jacob says you guys did a lot of things together. We were hoping to ask some questions as we try to find who may have done this to her."

"Oh. Yeah, sure. Come on inside."

"Is your wife home, by any chance?" Jack asked.

"Yeah. She's upstairs, in the office."

"You guys work from home?"

"We do. We run an e-commerce shop for pop culture items. Mostly vinyl, cassettes, and even some hard-to-find VHS tapes."

Kyle led them into a small living area but did not sit down. Instead, he angled his head back out to the hallway and called out up a flight of carpeted stairs. "Hey, Jill? Can you come down for a second?"

"Yeah, one sec…"

With that, Jack finally joined them. Jack studied the room, finding it quaint and modest. He also noted that there were several framed pictures sitting on the mantle over the gas-log fireplace.

"Jacob said they found her out in the desert, in the middle of nowhere," Kyle said. "Is that true?"

"It is," Jack said. "And she's not the first. Another woman was found in the same condition, in the desert. We may be dealing with a serial killer in the area, so any information you and your wife could give us would be very helpful."

This news seemed to stun Kyle. He remained standing in the archway between the living area and the hall. He ran a hand nervously through his long, brown hair, trying to process it all. At the same time, the sound of someone coming down the stairs could be heard as Jill Browning appeared.

"These are FBI agents," Kyle said, nodding to their guests "They want to ask us some questions about Valerie."

"Oh…"

Jill nodded slowly and joined Kyle by the archway. She was an attractive brunette, her lips full and her eyes bright. Yet within seconds of hearing why the agents were in their home, those eyes seemed to dim and her lips were cast into a frown.

"We went by to speak with Jacob," Rachel said, "but he was in no condition to talk. We saw a picture of you two on his fridge and figured we'd see if you could potentially be of some help."

"We can certainly try," she said. "We didn't know them *super* well."

"How did the four of you come to know one another?" Jack asked.

"We actually met at a trivia night at a bar," Kyle said. "That was about two years ago. Right?" He looked to his wife for confirmation.

"Yeah, about two years ago."

"Did you go hiking with them often?"

"Every now and then, yeah," Jill said. "Valerie really wasn't into the whole outdoorsy thing, but Jacob loved it, so she gave it her all."

"All we got from Jacob is that you guys did a lot of stuff together," Rachel said. "What else was there other than hiking?"

"Trivia nights, mostly," Kyle said. "That was sort of our thing. But we'd also just get together for dinner every now and then. Board games, a movie here and there, that kind of thing."

"And did they get along, for the most part?" Jack asked.

"Oh yeah." Jill smiled thinly, her eyes reflecting that she was deep in a memory. "I think I saw them seriously argue just one time, and that was over which wine to buy."

"Yeah, they were a legit couple," Kyle agreed. "And I feel just awful for Jacob." He looked over to his wife fleetingly and added, "I just can't imagine."

"Can either of you think of any reason Valerie may have been in any kind of trouble? Maybe with a disgruntled friend or family member?"

"No, but again, we didn't know them on a deep, personal level," Jill said.

"Do you happen to know if either of them were involved in any criminal activity, no matter how minor?" Jack asked.

He noticed almost right away that Kyle looked down to the floor at this. He also crossed his arms and pivoted on his feet a bit. He cut his eyes in Jill's direction, a clear indication that he *really* wanted her to answer this question.

"If they were," Jill said, "I never knew about it. I mean, we joked around sometimes about our younger years, you know? Stories about pot and things like that. But I never saw them doing any drugs. And in terms of other crimes, I…well, I just find it hard to even picture them doing anything illegal."

When she looked to Kyle to back her up on this, he still seemed uneasy. Still, he nodded and said "Yeah, that's right."

"You can't think of *anything* at all, Mr. Browning?"

A look of fear briefly crossed Kyle's face as he was individually singled out. Again, he looked toward Jill for just a split second but still shook his head. "No, sorry. I can't think of anything at all."

Jack watched as Rachel reached into her inner jacket pocket and fished out one of her business cards. She handed it to Jill as she made her way out of the room. "I think that's all for now," Rachel said. "But please, don't hesitate to call us if you think of anything. I don't care how small or inconsequential you think it might be."

"Sure, of course," Jill said. "Sorry we weren't any help."

Both of the Brownings escorted them to the front door. As Kyle held the door open for them, Jack eyed him once more as he walked out onto the porch. He and Rachel headed back out across the lawn, to the car. It wasn't until Jack reached for his door handle that he heard the front door closing behind them.

"Thoughts?" Rachel asked.

"I think Jill Browning is being truthful. But I also think Kyle was a bit guarded. Did you see how antsy he got when I asked about criminal activity?"

"I did," she said as she nestled down into the passenger seat. "You think it was maybe something he didn't want his wife to hear? Or maybe he just didn't want to say at all?"

"I don't know," Jack said. "He kept looking over at her, like he was trying to figure something out."

"Maybe we come back around to him later on—and next time have it just be him without Jill."

"If there *is* some sort of criminal activity," Jack said, "you'd think Duvall would have found it in the preliminary search for information."

He cranked the car and he was about to pull back out onto the street when he noticed Rachel wincing slightly. She let out a thin sigh and looked like she was cringing a bit.

"What is it?" Jack asked. "Are you okay?" He hated how panicked he sounded but was helpless to stop it. He'd asked the questions in an alerted voice before he was even aware he was going to ask them.

"Yes," she said. "I'm fine. It's just the heat, I think. Just a slight headache. The lack of sleep from last night isn't helping, either."

"You're sure?"

She let out another sigh, but this was an irritated one. "I'm sure, Jack. Not every single ache and pain is related to the tumor."

"I know, I just—"

Rachel's phone rang, and Jack could see the relief on her face, having been saved from a conversation she didn't want to have. She took the call quickly. "This is Agent Gift...yes, hello. Hold on, let me put you on speaker."

She sat the phone on the console and switched it over to speaker mode. "Okay, Agent Duvall, you're on speaker. Agent Rivers is here with me."

"Good. So, Jacob has just been admitted. Based on what the medics saw in the back of the ambulance, he should be fine. More than that, though, I got a call on the way to the hospital from one of the State officers that has been assisting with some background stuff. Remember, I told you I have a guy on the State PD diving into some of the social media accounts of the victims, trying to find any sort of link?"

"Yes."

"He found a single hit. He said the victims weren't friends—that they didn't follow each other on any platforms. But he did find one single friend they had in common."

"Just one?"

"Yeah. And if you have the time, I've got a name, phone number, and address for you."

"That's great," Jack said. "Let us have it."

Duvall gave them the address and Jack once again directed his car down sun-blazed streets to another house. It was almost enough promise and progress to make him forget about that unspoken threat sitting between him and Rachel, the tumor that was starting to feel like a third part of their team.

CHAPTER TEN

Rachel had become aware of the same fifty-fifty rate of people being home on weekdays that Jack had started to notice. However, when they reached the address of the common friend shared by Valerie and Malorie, it was another case of the person not being home. The person in question was named Maria Herrera, age twenty-five. According to what the police had found, the only criminal activity on her record were two parking tickets, both of which had been promptly paid. She lived on the second floor of a four-floor apartment building in Albuquerque, but apparently had a more traditional job that required her to be on-site.

In no hurry to get back outside in the heat of the afternoon, Rachel and Jack stopped in the small downstairs lobby. It really wasn't as much of a lobby as it was a simple square space that contained the mailboxes for all of the apartments, a few potted plants, a community bulletin board, and a two small love-seat sized chairs.

Rachel perched herself on the plush armrest of one of the chairs as she called the number Duvall had given them. It rang five times before clicking over to voicemail. The recording had not been personalized, so Rachel listened to a robotic female voice asking her to leave a message—which she did not.

"No answer," she said, ending the call.

"If she's at work, it could be a coincidence," Jack said. "Not everyone can answer their phones at work."

"Maybe. I wonder…would you mind calling Duvall to see if she could find out where Maria Herrera works? I'd like to check in with my grandmother. She's sort of watching Paige while I'm out here wandering around in the desert."

"Yeah, sure thing."

Rachel remained where she was, on the arm of the chair, while Jack walked to the other side of the lobby over by the mailboxes. She was certain Grandma Tate would be slightly irritated that she was calling to check in, but that was to be expected. And honestly, Rachel understood it. The way Jack was now treating her like she was this incredibly fragile porcelain doll helped her to understand what her grandmother must also be going through. But honestly, cancer or no cancer, Rachel would have called to check on them regardless.

Grandma Tate answered the call on the third ring and skipped right past the hellos and niceties. "For goodness sake, Rachel. She's at school. I'm fully capable of sitting here and waiting for the end of the day."

Rachel could easily sense the sarcasm. "Oh, well you wait until the car rider line at school."

"Car rider? She doesn't ride the bus?"

"No! You have to go—"

Grandma Tate's laughter from the other end of the line cut her off. "Oh, stop it! I know I have to pick her up. I'm leaving in about ten minutes to do that very thing."

"Did everything go well this morning?"

"Yes. She had to help me figure out how to run the coffee maker, but other than that, all is well."

"Has Peter tried calling?"

"I think he attempted to FaceTime her on the iPad. But I might have conveniently overlooked that."

"It's okay for him to talk to her."

"I know. I just didn't want to give him the pleasure."

"Well, thanks again for hanging in there for me. Don't get too upset if I manage to call again to talk to Paige before bedtime."

"As long as it's to say goodnight to her and not check up on me, that's fine. Now…tell me honestly, girl. How are you?"

"I'm good. It's just hot as hell out here."

"You're telling the truth?"

"I am. You have my word."

"Okay then. Be careful out there."

"Hey, I'd rather be here than about to get into the car ride line. *You* be careful."

They ended the call on that note. It left Rachel wondering how much longer she'd be able to pull this off—working with the tumor residing in her head. She was certain there would come a point where even if she decided to push as hard as she could, the tumor would just start shutting things down. How long before that happened, she wondered? Five months? Maybe eight at most?

She thought through all of this as she watched Jack pacing back and forth by the mailboxes, working on getting information on where Maria Herrera worked. He was speaking rather animatedly, making her assume they were coming to a dead end. After all, unless an individual had a dicey history, a current employer did not always show up on background checks or police records.

As she waited for Jack's call to end, her own phone rang. She did not recognize the number but realized the area code was the same as Duvall's. A local number. She answered it, wondering if maybe Kyle Browning had decided to fess up to whatever it was that had him feeling so uneasy during their visit.

"This is Agent Gift."

"Hello, Agent Gift. This is Shirly Baxter, the coroner. I found something in Valerie's bloodwork that I think might interest you. I'd called Agent Duvall first and she told me to call you instead."

"What did you find?"

"A decent amount of MDMA."

Ecstasy, Rachel thought, instantly bringing to mind Kyle Browning's reaction when they'd asked about any criminal activity in Valerie's past.

"Did Malorie have it in her bloodstream as well?"

"No. But Malorie did have trace amounts of LSD in her system." She hesitated here and then added, almost hesitantly: "It was in my report. Did you not get a copy of it?"

"Oh, no, I did. I'm sorry…just slipping up in the details, I guess." But was it just that? She *knew* she'd looked over Malorie Osborne's coroner report. Had she simply overlooked the part about LSD in the bloodstream? Or had she read it and—

Oh, are you really going to go there? she asked herself. Ironically enough, she heard it in Grandma Tate's voice.

She didn't want to go there but there it was all the same.

Had she read it and the tumor was starting to affect her memory? Hell, *would* the tumor start to affect her memory? It was certainly a question she needed to address with Dr. Emerson if she chose to visit him again.

"So, two victims with two different hallucinogens in their blood upon time of death," she confirmed.

"Yes, it looks that way," said Shirley Baxter. "Though, and I'm sure I don't need to tell you this, not all strains of MDMA cause hallucinations. But the amount in Valerie Mitcham's bloodstream indicates she would have probably had enough."

"Thanks for the information," Rachel said.

She ended the call just as it seemed Jack was starting to settle down. He hadn't ended his call yet, but his posture and lowered voice suggested it was close to over. Rachel thought about what this new discovery could mean. First of all, it cemented the fact that they needed to speak with Kyle Browning. Secondly, if both women had drugs in their system, she wondered if it poked a very large hole in their theory of rituals. If it had been the *same* drug, it would have maybe supported the theory, but being that it was different drugs…

Well, they're both hallucinogens, she thought. *Maybe there's something there.*

Before she had time to explore it deeply, Jack ended his call. As he walked over to her, he started shaking his head. "No luck. Just in case, I did go ahead and put the full order in, but you know how that goes."

By *full order* he meant a full glimpse at Maria Herrera's records. With just her name, the bureau would be able to pull just about everything on her, including social security number, last two known addresses, and last two known employers. It was a painstakingly slow process, though. It would likely be tomorrow morning before they got the information.

"Well, I got something," Rachel said. "A call from the coroner. Do you remember reading in Malorie's coroner's report that she'd had LSD in her system?"

"Yeah. Was it in Valerie's system, too?"

She felt a quick stab of doubt and fear when he confirmed that it had indeed been in the report—a report she'd read herself. But she pushed on, not allowing that gnawing feeling to wear on her too badly.

"No. Ecstasy. A decent amount, too. So, we now have two victims and two different hallucinogens. And I'm wondering if it had anything to do with why Browning started to look a bit nervus when you asked about criminal activity."

"We can maybe work up a plan to get them separated tomorrow," Jack said. "Maybe he'll speak when his wife isn't around."

"And maybe it might be worth our while to look into recent drug activity related to LSD and MDMA in the area."

"All good points," Jack said. "But at the risk of sounding lazy, I'd like to start putting all of this together from a hotel. I'm tired, I'm sweating my ass off, and I'm pretty sure Duvall should be kept in the loop on all of this, too."

She nodded, checking her watch and realizing that somehow, the day had indeed gotten away from them. She figured there was more they could do, but it was mostly looking into records or making phone calls—all things they could do from a motel room. Besides, there was her headache to consider. Maybe she needed to get off of her feet for a bit. She didn't even want to think about what it might be like to pass out in the desert—especially with Jack now constantly on the verge of babying her.

They marched back outside into the heat, carrying a variety of questions with them. And while there were not answers yet to be had, Rachel would rather have a dozen questions to ask than no leads or theories at all.

When she got back into the car, she made a point to look out of the window, away from Jack, when she closed her eyes and winced. There was a slight pain radiating along the right side of her head, almost like a pulsing sensation. And though she did her best to tell herself it was indeed just the heat, some deeper part of her heart doubted it.

And that little part was starting to get very worried.

CHAPTER ELEVEN

Rachel was mostly fine until they check into the hotel, and she saw the bed. The little catnap on the plane the night before had not nearly been enough. She was also pretty sure the heat had sucked a lot of the energy out of her. Seeing the bed, the idea of sleep became almost too much to ignore. But she knew if she laid down right then and there, the power nap she'd get would mess with a good night's sleep later.

So instead of a nap, she set up a little workstation on the side table by the bed. It was nothing more than her laptop, her phone, a pad and a pen she took from the bedside table drawer. With that set up, she closed the curtains, shutting away the bland parking lot of the meager hotel they'd selected right between Albuquerque and Foxham—which seemed to be the two focal points of the case so far.

She looked at the laptop, trying to think of anything she could do in regard to the case aside from looking through the same old case files. Curious, she placed a call to Duvall. She answered on the third ring and Rachel could hear a muffled murmur of conversation in the background.

"Hey there, Agent Gift. What can I do for you?"

"Well, first of all, please tell me you were able to get a ride from the hospital."

She chuckled and said, "Absolutely. One of the State guys showed up to take a statement from Jacob, so I caught him back. Did Shirley get in touch with you?"

Shirley? Rachel ran the name through her head, trying to draw up the face to match it. She had another split second of fear, wondering if her memory was starting to go and if it was a result of the tumor, but then she made the connection. Shirley. The coroner and part-time ME.

"She did. And that's part of the reason I'm calling. Is there any way for me and Agent Rivers to get remote access to the State PD database?"

"Yeah, that should be easy enough. When we end the call, I'll text you the information for the IT guy over there. What are you thinking?"

"I'm thinking I want to look over some of the more recent cases involving hallucinogenic drugs. Dealers, busts, anything. And if I can manage to cross reference them with violent crimes, it might give us a few leads."

"It's a good idea for sure, but it might be a bit harder than you're thinking. There are certain areas out in the desert where the use of psychedelics and hallucinogens are pretty common. It's used a lot for parties and basic recreation. Just a few weeks back, I made a bust where the perp had nine bags of mushrooms caps hidden beneath the passenger seat of his car."

"Thanks for the warning."

"Sure thing. Hold on and I'll send you that info."

They ended the call, and Rachel figured it was as good a time as any to grab a shower—not only to get the sweat of the day off of her, but hopefully to help wake her up and keep her alert for another few hours.

Under the water, she thought of the desert, wondering how many different ways a killer may see it as a sacred space—why it would be used as the site of what could have been a ritualistic murder. She knew there were plenty of Native American legends regarding the desert, but something about the removal of the heart and those odd halos of blood by the hands made her think this wasn't anything related to that culture. Of course, there was no way she could rule it out if they wanted to approach it from every possible angle.

Rachel felt refreshed when she stepped out of the shower, but not necessarily recharged. She was just *tired*. Checking her phone, she saw that Duvall had already sent the contact information for the IT guy to help set her up remotely. First, she checked her phone for nearby Thai places. When she unsurprisingly found there were none, she settled for pizza. As she waited for it to arrive, she called the number Duvall sent her and had remote access to the State PD records at about the same time the pizza arrived.

Duvall was right; there were far more reports centered on drugs than she'd expected. There were the usual busts for marijuana and cocaine, but the number of reports for MDMA, LSD, and DMT were much higher than she'd expected. DMT was becoming quite popular in the area from what she could tell. She knew a bit about it, primarily that it was being used in very small doses to treat certain mental maladies. However, when created organically and sold, it was, of course, illegal.

There were even a few drugs mentioned in the reports that Rachel had to run a Google search on: psilomethoxin, moxy, and jimscaline to name a few. But what she could not find was any sort of link between the use of these drugs and violent activities. She found one exception where a man taking DMT had punched a cop and broken his nose when he was apprehended right in the middle of his trip. When questioned later, the man claimed he was absolutely certain that the cop that went for him was a "machine elf" that was trying to tear his soul out.

What this told Rachel was that the killer himself was not likely using the drugs. She recalled that Duvall told her that there was a lot of drug use at parties within the area. It was very likely that the killer also knew this and was taking advantage of women that were using these substances. It was a good working theory, she supposed, and might actually create a fairly straight avenue to pursue.

With four slices of pizza gone and her eyes growing weary, Rachel checked the time and found that it had somehow come to be 8:15. She uttered a curse and picked up the phone to call Paige but then realized the time difference. It was after 11:00 back home, and both Paige and Grandma Tate would be fast asleep.

She looked at the notes she had scribbled down as she'd looked through the records. There were very few and as she'd dug deeper, each and every one had been crossed out. She looked at the bed and then at the time again. Maybe the shower *had* helped. Or maybe it was the pizza and keeping her mind active with the police records. Whatever the case, she knew sleep wasn't going to happen. Not yet, anyway.

With a sigh, she slipped on her shoes and headed for the door. On the way into the hotel lot four hours ago, Jack had pointed out the shady little restaurant on the other side of the lot, located about a half a block down where it was closed in on both sides by businesses that looked to have been out of business for a while.

A beer or two would put the blinders on, help her to get tired enough for sleep again. Without a good night's sleep, she was going to be insufferable tomorrow. So she headed out across the parking lot. She could feel the heat of the day still radiating from the pavement even though the night-time air was relatively cool. She followed the little glow of light from the restaurant window as she also glanced off to her left where, just behind the motel, the desert opened up like an infinite throat for the night. She was once again struck by the polarizing nature of it—somehow both beautiful and eerie all at the same time.

She came to the restaurant, a dusty little place called Rose's Grill, and stepped inside to find pretty much what she'd expected. The front three quarters of the place was set up like a respectable diner, complete with old-school booths and a few tall tables pushed against the wall. This area was separated by two long wooden steps that led to the bar area, which was separated from the dining area by a surprisingly charming lattice-style fence. The bar was currently occupied by seven people—and Rachel grinned when she recognized one of them.

She quietly approached Jack from behind as she slid up to the stool beside him. "I should have known I'd find you here."

Jack frowned playfully. "I'm not sure how to take that comment." He shrugged and sipped from his mug of dark beer. "Time differences have always screwed with me. No way I'd be able to sleep right now."

"Same...even though I was absolutely exhausted about four hours ago."

She flagged the bartender down, ordered what Jack was having, and settled in. She and Jack had spent a decent amount of time in this exact situation, having a few beers at the end of the day as they processed the shapes and edges of a case. But it felt different now and she knew it was because he knew about the tumor. She didn't want to admit it to herself, but there were going to be a lot of things that were different between them now. Yet, at the same time, she was glad he knew. It made her burden feel a bit lighter.

"I've been thinking about the hearts," Jack said. "Taking someone's heart is a pretty bold statement, wouldn't you say. Like, it's not as visually brutal as a beheading, but it's just as jarring, right?"

"Right."

The bartender brought her beer over and her first sip was a bit long. It went down far too easily and brought a bit too much relief. She was pretty sure she'd have to cap herself at one tonight or else she may not leave until she was swaying.

"So it's making me think the killer is definitely trying to express something," he went on. "Don't you think?"

"I do. You mentioned beheadings...and if you look back through history, there were a lot of armies that beheaded their enemies or scalped them as a means of keeping trophies. They took the heads and scalps and sort of displayed them to strike fear into their enemies. But I don't feel like that's what our killer is doing here. He's not just taking the hearts as trophies."

"Naked and stretched out on a rock...makes me think maybe he feels a level of intimacy with them. But neither body had been sexually abused in anyway. So if it *is* an intimacy thing, it must be purely emotional."

"And Valerie did have ecstasy in her system," Rachel pointed out. "A drug that heightens certain emotional states and feelings of pleasure. So maybe there's something there. I called Duvall and got access to the State PD system. There's a lot of reports filed for mind-altering drugs. I think out killer is targeting parties where he knows these drugs are being used and then striking when the drugs hit."

Lifting his mug to his mouth, he tilted it toward her in acknowledgement. "That's a good train of thought. My worry, though, is that he may be done. He may be gone and we're just sniffing around in the desert."

"Why's that?"

"I honestly don't know. Just a feeling I have. Something about the hearts—the empty chests, the huge, sprawling desert."

"See, to me, that indicates he might just be getting started."

"And I don't really care for either possibility," Jack said. He eyed her cautiously and sat his beer back down on the bar. "Sorry. I have to ask. Is it okay for you to drink?"

A sting of irritation passed through her, but she swatted it away with good old sarcasm. She took a large swig of her beer, set it down, and shrugged. "Until I have a doctor tell me otherwise, I'm assuming so."

"I'm just worried about you…"

"I know you are. And I appreciate it. But you're going to have to trust me on some of this stuff."

"Yeah, I know. I just need you to promise me one thing. And if you can make this promise, I'll do my best to stop being so pushy."

"What's the promise?"

"I need you to be self-aware. When you *know* the tumor is starting to wear you down—when you know it's affecting your mind, your body, the way you approach the job—you need to step down. Now just for me, but for your own safety."

She took another sip of beer, trying to figure out if she was offended or deeply moved by this. In the end, she decided it was a bit of both. But she nodded and looked him in the eyes with the sort of care and intensity she usually reserved for only her family.

"You have my word," she said.

That seemed good enough for Jack. He smiled and turned his attention back to his beer. It left Rachel wondering what it might be like to quit. Would it really rob her of so much? Was her identity so ingrained in her work that she'd feel like nothing without it?

She just didn't know if she'd have the courage to keep this promise. After all, the tumor had already caused her to black out a few times since she'd been diagnosed and now there were concerns about it affecting her memory.

Rachel hated to break promises of any kind but as she sat at the bar and nursed her beer, she wondered if that was something else the tumor might eventually take away from her.

CHAPTER TWELVE

He could feel the energy coming off of the bonfire, the crackling, the popping, the burning. It felt like a constant stream of thunder, vibrating through the air and right into his sternum. Some strange electronic music was blaring through a large, hidden Bluetooth speaker somewhere just behind the fire. These kids called it psybient, if he was correct. A mix of New Age ambient and old school rave music.

He wasn't on drugs, though he'd once done copious amounts of them and knew that the sensation he was currently feeling was similar to a few mind-altering drugs. Mushrooms, in particular. The best part of all, though, was that just about everyone else around that big fire was on drugs. A lot of drugs.

He'd been here for less than half an hour and had already declined ecstasy three times, mushrooms twice, and DMT once. While using DMT was indeed tempting, he knew he had to keep a clear mind. With a. clouded mind, he'd miss his calling—he'd miss his chance to take the next heart.

He scanned his surroundings, staring blankly out toward the massive bonfire as if he, too, were tripping. So many of them already were. There were three women sitting in a circle, giggling madly after having taken ecstasy. To his right and hidden just inside the vague darkness where the night started to take over the desert, a young couple had stripped out of their clothes and were running their hands slowly along one another. Probably ecstasy there, too.

None of them mattered, though. Not too long after he'd arrived here, he spotted the woman he wanted next. She was alone, sitting on the edge of a small boulder off to his right. He'd watched her take something in pill form not too long after first setting his eyes on her. She'd followed it up with half a joint which she dropped to the desert floor as the pills had taken her over.

She looked to be twenty or so. Surely no older than twenty-five. She was blonde, with a waifish build. Flat chested, long-legs. He assumed that some other man would likely start hitting on her when she was good and whacked out of her head. So he needed to get to her first. He had to time it right, though. He knew there was a magical point where they were still somewhat coherent but also suggestible and agreeable to most things. The good news was that he'd done this before. He'd become something of an expert at timing it just right.

She wasn't very pretty—not in the face, anyway. But he could sense her heart. She had a beautiful heart, a healthy heart.

And soon it would be his. She'd fight him a bit at first. They all did. But in the end, they seemed to understand what he was doing…that they were part of something bigger than their own lives. Usually, the last breath they drew in was used to sigh in relief. Their last glances at him were looks of gratitude.

They were all free and mostly happy when he unburdened them of their hearts and left them to the hungry spaces of the desert.

He watched as the thin woman's eyes grew hazier. Her head tilted. She ran her hands over her stomach, exposed by the very short tank top she wore. If she'd had breasts of any considerable size, the bottoms would be exposed. That's how short the shirt was. It's almost as if she'd dressed for the occasion, knowing that she would be offering up her heart to him before the night was done.

Slowly, he made his way to her. The energy from the fire and the night itself seemed to escort him gently in her direction. As he closed in on her, a young man wearing only a pair of very short biking shorts stumbled into him. Hs long black hair seemed to sink into the night, as if he were part of the night sky overhead.

"Hey, man," he said. His words were long and stretched out. His eyes sparkled with a sort of dull shine, and his legs swayed as if his bones had turned to jelly. "You…you need to try this."

He spoke in a way that sounded as if he might turn this simple statement into a song. In saying it, he reached out and took his hand as if they were lovers. It was a gentle but reassuring touch. The swaying man deftly placed a small bag of something into his hand.

Without even looking, he pushed the bag down into his pocket. From the feel of it, it was likely a mushroom cap. It wasn't solid or small enough to be a pill. Even though he didn't do drugs, he wasn't foolish enough to toss it to the floor. Having it on hand could be very beneficial to him in the future.

"Thanks," he said over his shoulder. But the flimsy young man was already scampering off elsewhere.

The girl was now about fifteen feet ahead of him, lying back on the boulder in a way that might have been sexy and alluring if he hadn't known that she was high. He wondered what she'd taken and what chemically induced sights she was seeing as he drew closer to her. He also noted that a few heads were turning in her direction—males that had not yet taken anything to slow their minds or curb their impulses. They looked like ghouls in the darkness, lurking and waiting to pounce.

He understood that he looked exactly like that, too. But he had a purpose. He had a mission and a reason that none of those lust-driven imbeciles would ever understand.

He hurried his step and approached her just as her eyes were starting to flutter closed. A light smile was on her lips as one of her hands ran slowly down her own neck, the other circling her navel.

"Hey, there," he said softly. "Are you okay?"

"Mmm. Yeeeeah…"

"I need you to listen. There are two men, right over there by the fire. They're planning something…something bad. And they keep looking over at you. Do you hear me?"

The smile on her face faltered a bit as she nodded. "Something bad?"

"Yeah. Come on and we'll get out of here."

Her eyes continued to flutter. He saw her brow furrowing a bit as she tried to sort it all out. He wondered if he'd come over a bit too early. He watched her hands running along her bare skin and assumed she'd taken ecstasy or some form of it, anyway. Slowly, he reached out and took the hand that was currently still grazing along her navel. He lifted it and ran his fingers along her palms, down her wrist.

The smile came back to her face and when he gently tugged at the arm, she got up. She swayed a bit, as if she'd just gotten out of bed, but when he placed an arm around her shoulders, she was agreeable enough.

"Something bad?" she asked.

"Well, I think it's okay now. We just need to get away from them."

When he had her off of the edge of the boulder and walking with him away from the campfire, he let go of her shoulders and took her hand again. He used his other hand to run his fingers up and down the length of her forearm. In many ways, it was like petting a dog to get it to do what you wanted. It made for some awkward walking but within a few minutes, the bonfire was nothing more than a flickering light behind them.

"Really tired," she said in a whisper. But she was giggling and leaning into him now. Whatever she'd take must have been quite strong.

"I think we're almost safe now."

"Safe?"

"Yes, and then I have something to show you. Something you're just not going to believe."

"How much...much farther? My feet are..."

"Want me to carry you?"

She giggled at this, but it was the only response. Knowing how pliable she would be in this condition, he stopped walking and swept her up. She let out a little gasp, but it was one of surprise and delight.

"So strong," she said. She placed her hand against his chest, her head cocked into his shoulder. He felt her running her fingers along his shirt. She made a soft purring sort of noise that he had to admit *did* make him start thinking of other things he could do to her.

At some point, she passed out on his arms. He felt her breathing, her frail weight next to nothing against his chest. He walked on, knowing exactly where he was going, wondering if she would wake up before then.

He arrived at the large, flat rock twenty-five minutes later. His arms had started to ache the slightest bit by the time he lay her down on the rock. As his arms came away from her and her head adjusted to the hard texture of the rock, her eyes lazily came open for a bit. He watched this as he reached beneath the crevasse on the right side of the rock, a small crack between the underside of the rock and the desert floor.

He'd stashed the knife there this morning, not wanting to run the risk of being seen back at the party—not that any of them would remember much of anything the next morning. That was another good thing about selecting his subjects from those particular parties. The drugs they took really messed with their minds. Any recollection they'd produce the following day under any sort of interrogation would be muddy at best.

"We here?" she said. "Wait...are we..."

She sat up. He brought the knife out and slashed it in a movement so fast that it surprised even himself. The blade tore through her throat and her eyes went wide as blood jettisoned out into the night. She opened her mouth and tried to scream but her throat had been severed.

She gasped. Blood came pouring out of her opened throat and over her lips.

After a few moments, she fell backwards.

He watched her die and gave the desert night a moment to appreciate the sacrifice.

Next, he climbed onto the rock with her and stripped her clothes off. He balled them up and placed them on the ground.

And then he went to work on her heart. He was ever so careful, using only the waning light of the moon. It took a good deal of time, as he did not want to nick the heart itself. Once he got started, it came almost naturally. And by the time he held her heart, still warm and soft, he could have sworn he could still feel it beating.

CHAPTER THIRTEEN

Rachel sat in a blindingly white room. There was no furniture, only her laptop, sitting on a floor that looked to be made of some sort of tempered seashell. The walls were featureless, reminding her of well-polished racquetball courts. The only thing that broke the monotony of the walls was a single door at the front of the room. It was large and made of glass. Three enormous hinges held it in place. As she stared through it, Peter stood on the other side, staring in.

"You should have told everyone," he said. "You should have told us from the start."

"I did. I—"

"But you waited so long. And now...now look..."

He stepped aside and Paige came into view. She was holding a scalpel, its edge stained with dried blood. "I can't trust you now, Mommy. Why couldn't you just tell us when you first found out?"

Behind her, Jack walked by, barely looking into the room. Director Anderson followed, looking in with great interest but then ultimately walking away. Grandma Tate came next. She stepped between Peter and Paige, resting a hand on her great-granddaughter's shoulder.

"You wanted to handle this all alone," Grandma Tate said. "So now you'll get it. Now you'll get exactly what you wanted."

One by one, they left the door. Paige was the last one to leave, staring in sadly. Eventually, she also moved along, dropping the scalpel as she did so.

"No...come back! Please..."

As Rachel started crawling for the door, she noticed her laptop. There were several tabs opened on it, all showing a police report in some form or another. One of them was a coroner's report and the name at the top was her own. Someone had taken a thick magic marker and scrawled the words MISSING HEART over the entire page.

"I'm sorry," she wailed to the glass door. "I should have—"

An abrupt knocking noise tore her out of her sleep. She sat up, gasping for breath and looking toward the door of the room. She then looked over to the clock on the bedside table and saw that it was 6:45. Apparently, she'd forgot to set an alarm.

The knocking at the door came again, this time followed by Jack's voice. "You okay in there, Rachel? Jesus, you only had a single beer last night."

She walked to the door, dressed in just a sports bra and a pair of athletic shorts. She opened the door a few inches and peered out. "I'm so sorry. I forgot to set an alarm. Can you give me like ten minutes?"

"Take twenty," he said with a shrug. "I'll head over to Rose's Grill and grab some coffee."

"You're a good man, Jack Rivers."

He gave her a thumbs up as she closed the door. Back in the darkness of the room, it was far too easy to recall the nightmare. Before she set about getting dressed and ready for the day, Rachel walked over to the laptop and put it into her workbag. It felt like a childish thing to do but it still made her feel much better all the same.

She went to the bathroom and splashed some cold water on her face before changing into her work attire. She was going to call Paige but once again, the time difference interfered. When she stepped outside to meet with Jack, she caught him already coming back across the parking lot from Rose's Grill. He was carrying two cups of coffee and when he handed her one, he did so cautiously.

"Fair warning: it smells like jet fuel and looks like sludge."

They got into the car, Jack getting behind the wheel. Even Jack, who drank his coffee just as dark and black as a moonless night grimaced a bit when he sipped from his coffee. When he sat it back down in the car's cupholder, he was still in shock from the potency of it.

"First thing on the day's agenda is to split up the Brownings," Jack said. "Any logical ideas?"

"Yes, actually. If Kyle truly was uneasy with the line of questioning and is hiding something, I think the chances are pretty good that he'd jump at the opportunity to have *just* his wife do the talking. Sort of lightens the load for him, right?"

"Yeah. I follow you so far."

"I think we get Duvall to call her. Say she's needed down at the station for some formal questions—nothing important, just some paperwork that needs to be filed away. She could even play the good guy role; she could say those assholes from the East Coast came in and made a bit of a mess and now there's some paperwork to be done about how she and her husband were questioned. Maybe she needs some clarification on their answers. And then while she's gone, we can just happen to pay Kyle another visit. Without his wife there, I really do think he'd be more open to telling us what had him so on edge yesterday."

"Sounds like a plan to me," Jack said, picking his coffee back up. "You got Duvall's number?"

"Already on it," she said, taking her phone from the center console. The phone rang only once before Duvall answered. She sounded incredibly chipper so early in the morning. Perhaps her coffee was of a better quality than what they'd gotten from Rose's Grill.

"Agent Gift, good morning. You guys on your way into the city?"

"We are. And we were hoping to get your help on pulling of a plan this morning."

"Absolutely. What have you got?"

Rachel told her and as she spelled it out step by step, she became more and more confident that it was going to work.

***

Rachel did the driving on the way out of Albuquerque when they left the precinct an hour and a half later. It was 9:10 when she parked their car at the edge of the block, facing the Browning residence just two houses down. They watched the house and waited for Duvall to text with confirmation that Jill Browning had arrived at the station.

"You think there's a chance Kyle Browning was having an affair with Valerie?" Jack asked. "Maybe that's why he was so antsy?"

"I don't know. Though…he didn't really start acting strange until Jill came down the stairs so maybe it's worth considering. But at the time, I figured it was because he didn't want to say something that he thought would piss her off."

As they both considered this, Duvall's text came through. **She's here. I'd say you have about an hour and a half.**

That's all they needed to hear. Rachel and Jack stepped out of the car together and walked over to the Brownings' house. Rachel noticed Jack going a bit out of his way to take the lead. They were both certain Kyle would be furious, clearly seeing that this had all been planned. If there was some anger or hostility, Jack wanted to meet it head-on before Rachel. She supposed she appreciated the gesture, but she couldn't recall him ever being so proactive about such measures in their pre-tumor partnership.

She said nothing about this, keeping a step back as Jack knocked on the door. There was a long enough pause to where she was sure Kyle Browning was not home. But just as Jack raised his hand to knock again, the door was answered. When Kyle saw them, his eyes went wide with confusion and then narrow with anger.

"Look…Jill is with Agent Duvall and some of the State PD guys right now, answering questions. What else could you possibly need?"

"Just some follow-up questions," Jack said.

"No, I don't think so. I think we've—"

Rachel stepped up, happy to interrupt. "You want the truth? What we really want to know is why you looked like a nervous little boy giving a presentation in front of class when your wife came downstairs—especially when we started asking about criminal activity."

He eyed them for a moment and the anger flared a bit, only to deflate down into something resembling resentment. "So you planned this?"

"Mr. Browning, can we come inside?" Jack asked, ignoring the question.

Kyle thought about it for a moment and then stepped aside, opening the door for them. He said nothing as they entered but took the lead and led them back into the same living area they'd visited yesterday.

"Were there any legitimate questions Jill needed to answer at the station?" Kyle asked, settling into the small couch against the far wall.

"A few, yes," Rachel said, not sure if this was true or not.

"Mr. Browning, at the risk of sounding conceited, both Agent Gift and myself are very good at our jobs. Your behavior when we asked about any illegal activities told us that you were keeping some things to yourself. Why is that? What was it that you did not want to talk about in front of your wife?"

Kyle was showing those same signs now, clearly uncomfortable while sitting on his own couch. "Will any of this *really* help you find Valerie's killer?"

"We don't know for certain, but there's a good chance," Jack said. "So let me start with this: would it surprise you to know that a medical exam following her death showed that she had MDMA in her system?"

"MDM…? You mean ecstasy?" He frowned and looked at the floor. He nodded slowly and when he looked back up to them, he seemed profoundly sad. "No, that wouldn't surprise me at all."

"Did she do it regularly?" Rachel asked.

"Depends on what you mean by regularly. I know she'd done it at least six or seven times. A few of those times, Jill and I were with her. That's why I didn't want to say anything about it in front of Jill. She's sort of embarrassed about it. She's from a really strict religious background. And grown woman or not, if her mother found out, she'd have a fit. Plus, you know, I didn't know if we'd get in trouble."

"Why would you?" Jack asked. "Did the four of you do it together?"

"Yeah, but just twice. We, uh, we did ayahuasca a few times, too— the four of us all together. The first time, it was during this really poorly organized sort of spiritual retreat. After that, it sort of became a thing, you know? We'd either go out into our back yard and do it at night or hike out to the desert and do it. After a while, we started running into other people out in the desert that were doing the same thing. We started getting invited to these parties and small get-togethers."

"Are we talking about the ecstasy or the ayahuasca?" Rachel asked.

"Both. Now, I never did ecstasy. Jill did a few times. But I think Valerie really liked it. She said it gave her more clarity than anything else she'd ever tried."

"When was the last time the four of you got together in this capacity?"

"Oh, it's been a while. Jill and I sort of stopped. I wouldn't go so far as to say that Valerie had a problem—not at all, actually—but I do think she was starting to rely a bit too much on it to make sure she was always in a pleasant mood."

"Do you happen to have any idea where she got her drugs?" Jack asked.

"I don't. But if you know where to go out in the desert on any Friday or Saturday night, you're going to run into people that sell it. Hell, some people give it away. Mushrooms, DMT, LSD, ecstasy…there's a whole peace-and-love hippie-style movement out here based around it all."

"And you never heard her or Jacob talk about where they got their supply?"

"No," Kyle said, deep in thought. "But you know, now that I think about it, she did mention owing someone some money for what she called 'a good time.' This was the last time we saw them. She wasn't freaked out about it or anything. She just mentioned it sort of in passing."

"How much money are we talking?"

"I don't recall. Five or six hundred, I guess. I know it doesn't seem like much…not enough to kill someone, right?"

Rachel didn't dare say such a thing, but she knew for a fact that people had been killed for much less—especially when drugs were involved. She started to feel a stirring of hope, the idea that this conversation might lead them to a very big answer.

"Kyle, would you happen to know if Valerie ever went out into the desert with anyone other than Jacob?"

"Maybe. Like I said, there were small groups sort of running into each other all of the time."

Rachel wasn't quite sure where to take the questioning from there. She figured they could always go back to Jacob if he was able to talk. Surely he would know if Valerie had other people she wandered out into the desert with to get high. Before she could form another question, her phone rang. When she saw and recognized Duvall's number, she excused herself. She walked out into the hallway and answered it.

"Hey, Agent Duvall. Are things going okay there?"

"Things are fine at the station. But I'm not there right now. I'm headed back out near Foxham—and you and Agent Rivers need to come, too. Another body has been found out in the desert."

CHAPTER FOURTEEN

The directions Duvall had given Rachel took them down a thin road that shot directly down what seemed like the very center of the desert. Looking at the location on her Maps app, Rachel figured the scene was only about eight miles or so away from where the last body had been found. She had to look at the map because even though she hated to admit it, every inch of this desert looked the same to her. The longer she was around it, the more she started to understand stories of people getting lost out here.

And, as such, it also helped her to understand why a killer might use it to dump bodies.

Rachel pulled their car to the side of the road when Duvall's came into view. She parked behind the car and then she and Jack got out. They started walking directly to the north, as Duvall had instructed.

Jack uttered a curse as he looked out to the sun. "Anderson really should have warned us about this. I don't recall him saying we'd be wandering around in the desert the entire time we were here. Did you happen to catch that?"

"Nope. Must have missed it."

As it turned out, though, Duvall's directions were pretty spot-on. They only had to walk a total of five minutes before they came to where Duvall and a local officer were standing. As they approached, Rachel looked back toward the road and realize she could still see the hazy shape of the cars.

"How was this one found?" Rachel asked.

"Local PD got a call from a man living just outside of Albuquerque," Duvall said. "He was out doing fly-bys with a drone, catching some stock footage of the morning desert. He was about half a mile *that way*," she said, pointing to their right, "when the body came into view."

Rachel looked to the ground and was almost floored by how identical the set-up looked to the others. The body had been placed on a slight protrusion of stone from the desert floor. Arms outstretched, stripped nude, heart removed. The only real difference was that this site was much fresher than the others she'd seen. It was more visceral, grislier. The blood gleamed in the morning sun and the cavern where her heart had once been seemed almost black. The girl looked somewhat waifish and had a small tattoo of a frog on the left side of her hip.

"Do we have an ID yet?" Jack asked.

"We do," Duvall said. "And you're not going to like it. I knew who it was right away because I'd been trying to help locate her all of yesterday afternoon, at your request."

Rachel looked away from the body, directly to Duvall, hoping she was misunderstanding her. "Are you saying this is Maria Herrera?"

"I am."

"Damn," Rachel said. Maria Herrera, the one solid link they had between Valerie and Malorie. The one person they'd been unable to get in touch with yesterday, someone to provide potential answers. And now she was dead. Not just dead but taken in the same manner as the other two victims.

"You think it was intentional?" Jack asked. "Maybe the killer is hand-picking his victims from one group of people?"

"Could be," Duvall said.

Rachel made her way slowly around the out-cropping of rock. She began to make several speculations, some simple and others a little off base. First of all, all three victims had been placed on a stone that seemed to be serving as an altar. Each stone had been large enough to lay a body on, fully stretched out. And so far, the bodies had all been displayed within about a twenty-mile range.

"He's planned it all out," she said. "These aren't just random killings. He knows the locations he's going to display the victims before he kills. And if he's being particular enough about the locations, I assume he's being choosy about his victims."

"So maybe he *is* targeting a specific group," Jack said.

Rachel nodded. She thought of something Kyle Browning had said yesterday—about how if you knew where to look out in the desert at night, you'd run into little groups of people. People that were partying and, according to Kyle, probably doing drugs of some kind or another.

She looked at the officer that had come with Duvall. "Did anyone bother to get the footage from the drone this morning?"

"We did. He sent it right to the department."

"How long is it?"

"Just a ten second clip, showing where the body comes in. Why?"

"I think we need to get the full footage from him," Rachel said. "Everything he took this morning. We need to look for clues of small parties or get-togethers in the desert anywhere hear here."

"I can do that," the officer said. He was a middle-aged man with weary eyes and skin that showed signs that he'd lived here all his life—slightly red and almost leather-like. Still, he looked rather excited to have something to do.

Rachel stepped close to the rock, close enough so that Maria's left hand was nearly touching her pants. There seemed to be more blood splatter on the rock and the surrounding ground than from the other sites. Of course, that could be because this was the first time that she'd ever seen one of the sites so soon after the murder had been committed.

Jack came up beside her and hunkered down to have a look as well. When he spoke, he did so softly. Rachel assumed this was because he didn't want Duvall to hear them having anything resembling an argument.

"Something else to consider," he said. "All three bodies have been nowhere near towns or cities or even houses, from the looks of it. The killer is bringing them out here. Or luring them. And either way, I'm still hung up on the set up of it all."

Rachel nodded, looking to Maria's still-opened eyes. Why would three women willingly follow someone out into the desert at night? She could only think of two reasons: they either knew the killer and trusted him, or they were high. And Jack was right. If they weren't being lured, they were being killed elsewhere and then carried out here. And that would likely take the strength of more than just a single man—especially to leave no traces of dragging or struggle.

"You're still thinking it's a cult?" she said.

"I am. I think it might not hurt to start approaching things as if I'm right."

"I can agree to that." She stood back up and looked out into the desert, looking for any further blood trails or kicked up dirt. But there was nothing. "Has the family been contacted yet?"

"We tried, but from what we can find, there is no family. No record of a father at all, and the mother passed away a few years back. The only person we had to inform was her roommate and, according to said roommate, also best friend. A twenty-six-year-old named Abagail Tremont."

"So far, psychedelic drugs are the only link between the other two victims," Rachel said. "As soon as humanly possible, we need to have Ms. Herrera tested for narcotics."

"I already put that request in," Duvall said. "The coroner is on the way right now and I've already put in that instruction."

"Good. Agent Duvall, unless you have an issue with it, I'd like to speak with the roommate."

"Of course."

"We have an officer over there with her right now," the officer on the scene said. "Last I heard, which was about three minutes before you showed up, she's handling it remarkably well. Just a little shocked."

"Agent Duvall, I wonder if you can maybe do me a favor," Rachel said. "I don't know if it would require bureau resources or just local PD. But I wonder if you can maybe talk with some of the folks we've already questioned and use whatever you find to hunt down potential drug dealers. If Ms. Herrera does come back positive, that's three women that all knew one another. I'd assume they share the same dealer."

"I can absolutely do that."

Rachel looked back down to the body of Maria Herrera. This woman had very likely been alive just five or six hours ago. The killer had come in and taken her heart, taken her life, and had left no clues behind. It was ritualistic without a doubt and the harder she thought about it, the more she wondered if Jack *was* right. Maybe it was a cult or, if not an actual cult, someone that was wrapped up in some warped sort of quasi-religious philosophies.

"You good here, to wait for the coroner?" Rachel asked.

"Yeah. And I'll let you know if I find anything from my search."

Rachel and Jack both nodded their thanks and turned back toward the road. The cars twinkled brightly in the distance, reflecting the sun. Rachel spotted a third car now and, within another thirty seconds, saw the moving shape of a woman coming across the desert. As they grew closer, she recognized the face of Shirley Baxter, the coroner that worked out of the basement of the Foxham police department.

"Same as before?" Baxter asked.

"Identical," Jack answered.

"Well then, I suppose I might be seeing you two later. Be safe out there, agents."

They passed by and Rachel once again felt the overwhelming vastness of the desert. The open space of it all felt almost oppressive, and she couldn't get away from the feeling until she was back in the car.

CHAPTER FIFTEEN

When they arrived at the apartment building this time, Rachel felt a sense of more pressure—not only because they were speaking with someone very close to the most recent victim, but because another body meant they were dealing with a killer that seemed to be getting more blatant. He could literally kill again at any moment, even though it so far seemed he preferred to strike and do his work at night.

At the same time, she couldn't help but feel slightly disconnected. Had it really been just yesterday that she and Jack had visited this building in the hopes of speaking with Maria Herrera? She wrestled with this as they took the stairs to the second floor, trying to get a grasp on the fluid passing of time during a case like this; the passing of time, after all, had become a much more concrete thing to her ever since she'd gotten her diagnosis.

When Jack knocked on the door to the apartment, Rachel was surprised when it was answered not by the attending cop, but by a red-eyed young woman. She didn't look sad, though, necessarily. If anything, she looked a little angry.

"Are you Abagail Tremont?" Rachel asked.

"I am. You the FBI agents they said were coming?"

"We are."

"Come on in, then," Abagail said.

She let them in, the front door opening directly into a tidy kitchen. She saw why Abagail had answered the door, as the cop that had come by to break the news and get her details was currently talking on his cellphone over in the adjoined living room area. He gave them a quick wave of acknowledgement but remained on the call.

"You guys know any more than the cops do?" Abagail asked. She sat down at the small, round kitchen table and sipped on a mug of tea that was there, waiting. Steam still drifted up from it.

"No," Rachel said. "And that's why we're here. We need to ask some questions and I apologize ahead of time if they're ones the cops already asked."

"It's fine." She nodded to the cop in her living room and said, "He got that call about a minute ago. Apparently, they're trying to get the drone that got the footage of her body."

"Yes, that's right," Jack said. "We're hoping more footage than what was originally provided might give us some leads."

"Abagail," Rachel said, "when was the last time you saw Maria?"

"Last night. Maybe around ten or so, I guess."

"What sort of mood did she seem to be in?"

Abagail shrugged and sipped from her tea. "Normal. Not in a bad mood, but not like overly happy. Just regular."

"And did she tell you if she had planned to go out last night?"

"She mentioned maybe going out to dance with some other friends of hers."

"Do you know where?" Jack asked.

"No. I don't do that whole dancing scene. Maria had had her own little circle of friends for that. Clubs, music, dancing."

Without being invited to do so, Rachel sat down at the table. "Did Maria do drugs very often?"

The question seemed to baffle Abagail. She even looked at Rachel as if the idea seemed preposterous. "Maria? No. I mean…not as far as I know. And we knew each other really well. I feel like that's something I would have known. She wasn't like a teetotaler or anything. She'd have a glass of wine with me every now and then and I know she smoked pot a few times in college. But, no. I can say pretty confidently that she wasn't doing drugs."

"How about these other friends of hers? The ones she went dancing with?"

"I don't know. But I'd be surprised if they did. If they *did* and Maria knew, I don't think she'd be hanging out with them."

"Would you happen to know any of these other friends?"

"No. I know there were three of them, but she never brought them around here. She did it out of respect for me; I'm a pretty big introvert."

"You never heard names at all?" Jack asked.

"I'm pretty sure there was one named Amy. I don't know a last name, though."

"How often did she go out dancing with this other group of friends?" Jack asked.

"Maybe once or twice a month."

Rachel was about to ask another question, but the cop in the living room was suddenly walking quickly in their direction. "Ms. Tremont, did you and Maria happen to have the Find My Phone feature activated on your phones?"

She grinned at first but then took on a very serious look. "We did! We turned it on last year when we went to Disneyland and never turned it off. We always joked that by leaving it on, we'd know where to come pick the other up of we ever got lucky with a guy."

As Maria got up and walked to the kitchen counter to retrieve her phone, the cop gave Rachel and Jack something of a disappointed glance. "It's a long shot. But the guys with State PD noted that the other victims' phones were found in the pockets of their discarded clothes, not too far away from the bodies. That wasn't the case with Maria."

It was the sort of break that seemed to come from nowhere. Rachel knew better than to get too excited, though. Even if they could find it, there was the matter of unlocking it. And that was going to require a technician to get involved or, God help them, the phone company. In other words, even if it netted answers, they'd be a long time coming.

Only, when Abagail told the feature on her phone to locate the position of Maria's phone, they heard a soft pinging noise right away. They all looked in the direction the noise was coming from—toward the living room and off to the right.

"What the hell?" Abagail said.

She got up and hurried after the noise. Rachel and Jack followed, the cop trailing behind. They followed Abagail down a short hallway and into one of two bedrooms. The blinds to the room were closed, leaving it in a musty sort of darkness. The room, like the rest of the apartment, was very tidy. The bed was made, the small work desk next to the bed was cleaned and well-organized, and the entire room smelled of faint perfume.

The dinging was coming from the little work desk. It sat beside a laptop, pinging away. Abagail ran to it and when she picked it up, she held it out as if she thought she might be holding a bomb.

"That's Maria's?" Jack asked.

"Yeah," Abagail said, staring oddly at the phone.

"Did she normally leave it at home when she went out?"

"No. Not that I know of. I mean, I don't think so."

"Any chance you know her password?" Rachel asked.

Abagail nodded slowly, finally snapping out of her surprise and confusion to shut the Find My Phone alarm off. She pocketed her own phone and then tapped the lock code in for Maria's. If nothing else, Rachel thought that Abagail knowing Maria's password backed up the idea that the two had been very close.

When the phone was unlocked, Abagail handed it over to Rachel. Rachel instantly opened up Maria's text messages, looking for an Amy. She found it right away and found evidence that leaving the phone behind may have been totally accidental. There were nine messages in a row, all unread, that showed Amy asking where Maria was. *Yo bitch, we all here. Where you?* That was the first one. The rest were variations of the same question. The last one was sent at two in the morning and read: *Better have a good reason for bailing. C ya tomorrow.*

"She never showed up to meet her friends," Rachel said. Looking back to Abagail, she asked, "You said you last *saw* her at ten. Were you still awake when she supposedly left?"

"I was probably awake, yeah. But I was watching TV in my room. I never *heard* her go out, so I don't know an exact time."

"Who else other than this other group of friends would she have possibly met up with?" Jack asked.

"I...I don't know." Abagail seemed hesitant in this answer. Rachel didn't think she was lying, per se, but she didn't think she was getting the entire truth, either.

"Was she dating anyone?"

"N...No. Dating, no. But she..."

"What is it, Abagail?" Jack asked.

"Well, she had this sort of secret relationship. Not even a relationship, really. Maria...well, she was going through something. She came to terms with the fact that she was gay last year. She'd been seeing this one woman, but it was nothing serious. She was just sort of testing the waters. That was how she put it."

"What's this woman's name?"

Abagail looked around the room at the three law enforcement members. "This—will this get back to her parents? She was *terrified* of what her mother might think of her."

"No. It doesn't have to come up."

"The girl's name is Robin. Again, I don't know a last name. I think they'd been dating or whatever for a few months, but Maria only mentioned her a few times."

"Did you ever meet her?" Jack asked.

"No. Maria brought her over here once, but I was out of town."

Rachel scanned through the texts and quickly found a thread with a contact with the name Robin. The most recent exchanges were from last night.

At 9:21, Robin sent: *If it's too late, I get it. Could be fun tho. I think they're good people.*

Maria's response: *No, I'm good. See you around 10:30.*
Same place?
Sounds good. Can't wait.
Do me a favor?
What?
Wear that raspberry Chapstick. I love tasting it on your lips.
STAHP!

There was provocative back and forth which Rachel started to feel slightly uncomfortable reading. She skipped some of it and read just the last few messages. It was quick dialogue wherein Maria told Robin she was heading out. But, just like Amy, there was another stream of unanswered messages from Robin. The last one was sent around midnight.

"And you never saw this woman?" Rachel asked again.

"No! Why? What is it?"

"Do you know anything about her?"

"I don't think so. I think…I'm pretty sure she's a health nut. I think Maria met her one day when she was doing yoga at one of those small studios."

Rachel opened up Maria's Facebook account, ignored all the notifications, and went straight to her friends list. She typed Robin into the search field and got two results. One was for a local coffee shop named The Robin's Nest. The other was for a woman named Robin Meeks. Rachel clicked on the little thumbnail and was taken to the profile.

Robin Meeks lived in Albuquerque and was a co-owner and teacher of a yoga studio. Her profile picture showed her in a very elegant pose.

"Well, seems like a match at first glance," Rachel said. She noted the address of the yoga studio and started to look through the woman's pictures. There weren't many, and she did not see any pictures of Maria.

What she did, see, though, were pictures of Robin Meeks with her husband and a son of about four or so.

"Maybe not," she breathed.

"Or maybe it's her exactly," Jack said. "Maybe it wasn't just being gay that Maria was afraid of being fully honest about."

It was a very good point. She typed the name of the yoga studio into her own phone and then handed Maria's phone back to Abagail. "Thank you for your help," Rachel said.

"Did you find something?"

"We don't know yet," Rachel said. And then, turning to the cop, she asked, "Do you know Agent Duvall?"

"I do."

"Could you please place a call to her and have her dig up a home address for a Robin Meeks? Let her know we're already heading to her place of business. Let her know we'll call her with any relevant updates."

The cop didn't seem thrilled with taking such instructions, but he nodded all the same. Once again, Rachel tried to tell herself not to get too excited. But as they made their way back down the stairs to the lobby, she couldn't help but wonder—if Maria had indeed been involved romantically with a married woman without Abagail knowing, what else had the young woman managed to hide?

CHAPTER SIXTEEN

The room was lit only by the glow of his laptop, and that's the way he preferred it. This secondary room in the basement, hidden away beneath the stairs, had recently become his favorite room in the house. When he purchased the house several years ago, he'd been told this little space had been intended as a storage area. But he'd had an electrical outlet wired to it and had been using it as a study. No windows. No light. No outside stimulus. Just the dark, dank room and the ghostly glow of his laptop.

That glow revealed a tiny room with no furniture to speak of. There was the old office chair he was sitting in and a well-worn bookcase along the back wall. He sat in the chair, laptop perched on his knees, and scrolled through various social media accounts. He was looking for a certain something—for a certain someone. This was the only real work he'd done for the past month or so and he was getting very good at it.

All around him, the cheap sheetrock walls were adorned with bizarre symbols he had drawn with either paint, markers, or, in one instance, his own blood. Some of them weren't visible in the dimly lit room, but he knew they were there. He remembered putting every single one of those markings up. He knew what each one meant— symbols and runes that he'd gathered here and there over the years.

The only wall not covered with the symbols was the one directly behind him. The bookcase that occupied most of this wall was filled with books, so many that they were crammed in so tightly it was hard to get them out. Well-worn spines faced out of each shelf, with the exception of the bottom right corner shelf. There, he had stuffed several of his journals. He'd started writing about his new task ever since the very first day it had been revealed that he had a gift waiting for him. He'd catalogued it, often using his own words as a way to process the weight of the gift he was working towards.

He felt those pages behind him just as he felt each and every one of the markings on the wall. Each page was a memory of how he'd come to this place, to this very moment. And it was a moment that had him thrilled. He wasn't sure *when* it would come to pass, but he felt like his work was nearly done. The gift he'd been searching for was nearly his.

He could feel it in the stagnant air of the room. More than that, he'd been feeling it all day—in the very air he pulled into his lungs, in the way the earth cradled his feet when he walked. It was as if the universe was preparing him for it.

And he was ready.

He just needed to find one more woman. Maybe two. He wasn't sure yet. He needed to find a fitting archetype to continue the work. It was actually rather easy. It came down to common friends on social media platforms, women that had similar groups and interests, similar lifestyles. And in this wretched age, when most women in their twenties felt an insatiable need to share every waking, breathing moment of their lives online, it made his work very easy.

With easy work like this, it was becoming apparent to him that the universe *wanted* him to succeed. The gift was his already—it was just a matter of finishing the work and claiming it.

He was being rewarded for his fervent study, for his patience. He was starting to feel that he may have been so obedient and devoted to his work that the gift may turn out to be more than he imagined.

He may end up doing so much more than prolonging his life. He could potentially become immortal.

Yes, he knew it was a conceited thought, but he was just so *in the flow* of everything that it was easy to imagine. Besides…just like the journals behind him and like the symbols scrawled on the walls, there were other things in his dark den that also seemed to sing to him, letting him know the time was near.

He could all but hear the voices of the three women he'd claimed so far. Their voices sang out to him and the universe beyond from the jars that sat atop his bookcase.

Three jars, each of which contained a heart.

They sang songs of gratitude to him. They thanked him for allowing their hearts to be part of a ritual that was going to please the universe.

Those hearts and the women that once possessed them were cheering him on. And as his eyes finally landed on his next victim on the glowing laptop screen, their choruses elevated, and for a moment he thought he could hear their hearts vibrating inside the glass.

Yes, he was going to be immortal. He just had to keep going, keep working towards the work that had been assigned to him.

Nothing could stop him now.

CHAPTER SEVENTEEN

Rachel and Jack arrived at the yoga studio just shy of one o'clock in the afternoon, right before a small class began. The studio was a small space but was set up in a very charming way that even Rachel couldn't help but admire. It had a minimalist feel, the lighting was perfect and even the New Age music seemed soothing to her, even though she typically detested the genre.

As they walked into the lesson space, which was located behind a thin wall of cool marble, Rachel spotted Robin Meeks up front, speaking to one of the nine people that had arrived for the one o'clock session. Robin's hair was up in a cute bun, and she seemed to have lost a bit of weight when compared to the pictures Rachel had seen on Facebook, but she was quite sure it was the same woman. The other instructor was off to the far side of the building, sitting at a small counter that was pushed against the marble wall.

Rachel discreetly approached the counter and, without saying anything at all, showed the other co-owner her ID. Rachel had just enough time to see the woman's look of shock and surprise. Rachel felt the woman watching as she and Jack made their way to the front of the studio space. She still had her ID out but held down by her side. Rachel was never a fan of blatantly letting all bystanders know that the FBI was taking away someone in the same room. When possible, she tried to remain discreet.

So when she stepped up to Robin Meeks, she made sure to show her back to the rest of the room. When she very quickly flashed her ID at Robin, no one other than the other co-owner had any idea what was going on.

"You're Robin Meeks, right?" Rachel asked.

"I…yes, I am." Her look of shock was much stronger than the other owner's. "Is there something I can do for you?"

"Yes. We actually need to speak with you in private. Is there a room here we can use?"

"Can it wait? I'm about to start a class." But her eyes kept going back to the ID, even as Rachel started to place it back into her pocket.

"I'd really rather not wait. What we have to talk about is a very time sensitive matter."

Robin nodded, and Rachel noticed that she looked very confused. There was very little fear in her expression, but she had clearly been caught off guard. It was enough to make Rachel quite certain she was being genuine. "Sure. Let me see if I can get Jen to fill in for me. You can…there's a little lounge area in the back. Hit the hallway and take the right. It's the last room on the hallway. I'll meet you there."

Rachel and Jack gave her a moment to check in with the other co-owner, heading back to the lounge area Robin had mentioned. The New Age music followed them through overhead speakers and the same calming aesthetic flowed throughout the place. It may have been the oddest place Rachel had ever visited while chasing leads and answers for a murder investigation.

The lounge offered a small loveseat and two plush armchairs. Rachel and Jack opted for the love seat, a tactic to help them appear as a unified force. "She didn't look like she'd been caught," Jack said. "Did you notice that?"

"What do you mean?"

"When she saw the FBI was here, she looked bewildered…not guilty. I didn't see an *oh shit* look on her face."

"Same. But really, all we have to accuse her of is cheating on her husband." And while this was true, she had to admit that the fact alone had skewed her opinion of the woman. But based on everything she was seeing up close and personal, she strongly doubted Robin had anything to do with the killings.

Jack was about to reply but that's when Robin came walking into the room. She closed the door behind her and eyed them both as she took a seat in one of the armchairs.

"You'll have to forgive me," Robin said. "It's not every day that FBI agents come into your place of business. I mean…what is this about? Is everything okay?"

"Not really," Jack said, doing his best to take the lead. "We're in town looking into a series of murders and we believe the latest victim is someone that is close to you. We got your name from her phone and—"

Robin's hand instantly went to her mouth, as if to hold in a cry. Her eyes instantly started to well with tears. Without removing her hand, she said: "Maria. It's Maria, isn't it?"

Jack could only nod for a moment. Robin cried into her hands, doing her best to keep it quiet. She took a few large, hitching breaths and eyed them with a deep and profound sadness. "So I suppose you know about…about *us?*"

"We know you were involved in some way, yes," Rachel said, trying to sound as compassionate and caring as she could. "But that's not why we're here. What I *would* like to know is how you knew right away it was Maria."

"We were…we were supposed to meet up last night," she said. Her voice was thin and tight as she tried to keep from breaking down completely.

"And she never showed?" Jack asked.

"No. And I didn't try to…try…I'm so sorry. Give me a second."

"It's okay," Rachel said. "Take your time. I know it has to come as a blow."

"Yeah, and…you said she was a victim of a murderer?" Again, her voice was tight and thin. That and the heavy, labored breaths was going to add up to a potential blackout of they weren't careful. She'd seen people act dramatically before, going so far as to fake asthma and panic attacks. But she remained confident that Robin's reactions were sincere. No one was that good of an actor.

"Yes," Rachel said. "And she's the third one. Listen…Robin, we're not here to ask about the romantic relationship between you two. Right now, we're trying to find out some information about her private life—things that her roommate and friend didn't even know."

"Like what?" Robin asked, wiping tears from her cheeks and eyes.

"We need to know if she was into drugs. Right now, psychedelic drugs are the only solid connection we have between the first two victims. If we can confirm that Maria used them, too, that could go a very long way to helping us establish something of a lead."

"We…well, yeah, sometimes. I met her here, at the studio and things just sort of escalated and it became a party thing. She never did hard drugs. No coke, no heroin, and hated the smell of pot. But she'd do psychedelics from time to time."

"How often?" Jack asked.

"Not too often. Not to be crude but our time together was always fleeting. We had to keep it a secret, you see. So most of the time, we got together and there were no drugs or parties. Just each other." She took a moment to collect herself. She looked ashen in the face, and she was still actively crying, but she seemed to have control of herself for now.

"And what about the times there was more?" Jack asked.

A sad-tinged smile came to Robin's mouth. "On occasion, my husband would leave town for work. I'd get a sitter and then Maria and I would go to those raves in the desert. It was sort of like dating, but no one we knew would see us, you know? And it was there, during those raves, where she'd do drugs. Mostly just a few tabs of acid. Some specialized kind. Not sure what it was, really. She would also do DMT. But again…these times were few and far between."

"Did she have a dealer?" Rachel said. "Or maybe not even a dealer—just someone she relied on to get the drugs?"

"I'm not sure, really. I don't think so. I mean, people are very liberal with the drugs they have at these raves. Sometimes it's very easy for women to get them for free."

A small flicker of realization popped up in Rachel's head. *A party atmosphere in the desert where young women have easy access to free drugs…seems like a very good place for a killer to abduct female victims.*

"Okay, so let's take a step back," Jack said. "How did you two even know where these raves were? Aren't they sort of invitation only?"

"Some are. Some start by one or two people sharing a location—sometimes even pinning it on Google maps and texting it out. But the ones Maria and I went to were a bit more inclusive. There was a text chain. I had somehow gotten on it when a client here at the studio included me a few months back—just because we got on the topic of mushrooms. So whenever I'd get a ping for them and my husband was out of town, I'd let Maria know."

"Do you have any of those texts on your phone right now?" Rachel asked.

"I don't know. I think there might be one from a few weeks back. Hold on." She got up and crossed the lounge area, opening a small cabinet where her purse had been stored.

"Last night, were you and Maria planning to go to one of those raves by any chance?"

Robin shook her head as she pulled out her phone. "No. We were just going to meet up."

"Is your husband out of town?" Jack asked.

"No," Robin said, with a bit of shame in her voice. "I was going to make a big production about how I'd forgot to pick up coffee and that I needed to run to the grocery store. But only if Maria could make it out. She said he would but she never showed up."

"So you'd just meet in the parking lot, and…" Jack asked. He apparently chose not to finish the thought.

"Yes," Robin said quickly, scrolling through her texts. "In her car. Sometimes, it was all we could get, but we'd gladly take it." Then, as if glad to change the subject, she held out her phone. "Here's the last of those texts that I received."

Rachel opened up the initial text and saw that it had been sent out to sixteen people. She was surprised to see that the sender didn't go to any lengths to keep their identity hidden. The phone number that initiated the text chain was a basic one, with a local area code.

"Do you know who sends them out?" Rachel asked.

"Not really. I've seen him at the raves, of course, but I never spoke to him. Now that I think of it, I don't even know his name." She eyed Rachel and Jack, that sullen sadness coming back into her eyes with full force. "Does this help?"

"It very well could," Rachel said, using Robin's phone to send the number to herself. She handed the phone back when she was done and though she felt silly saying it, considering the situation, she said: "I'm sorry for your loss."

The comment seemed to sit odd with Robin as she sank back into the armchair. "You don't need to tell anyone, right? About me and Maria?"

"No, I don't see why we would," Rachel said.

"Thank you. I know what you must think of me. But I love my husband and my son very much. But Maria…she was unexpected. She was fun and exciting and…well, she was special."

She started to cry again, burying her head in her hands and finally letting out one huge wail.

"Thank you, Mrs. Meeks," Rachel said. "We'll leave you to process it all."

She hated to deliver bad news and she especially hated walking out on the recipient of bad news. But given that there was an affair involved in this situation, she felt it was in everyone's best interest if she and Jack stepped out. Besides, they had a case to focus on, and a phone number that might take them to their first substantial lead.

CHAPTER EIGHTEEN

Rachel placed a call to Agent Duvall, asking her if she could work with the local PD to get a name and address for the number she'd taken out of Robin's phone. This was done before they even got back into their car. The afternoon was winding on, and the heat felt oppressive yet again. She couldn't imagine working a beat in this miserable heat, especially on a case like this one that continued to lead her out into the desert.

As Rachel got behind the wheel of the car, she set her phone on speaker mode. Within seconds of buckling her seat belt, Duvall's voice was speaking into the car. "Okay, so I got a name and an address for that number. Brett Alvarez, and he lives in Foxham. I'm texting you the address right now."

"I'm really getting tired of making this little jaunt between Albuquerque and Foxham," Jack said.

"I know, right?" Duvall said. "And the scenery all starts to look the same, too, right?"

"Eh, I haven't gotten tired of it yet," Jack commented.

"Agent Duvall, would you mind checking to see if Mr. Alvarez has a record of any kind?"

"Sure thing. I'll get back to you as soon as I get something."

They ended the call and Rachel pulled directions to Alvarez's place up on her phone. She was really enjoying having access to a third agent and not having to deal directly with the local PD. She rather wished she had an Agent Duvall on all cases going forward.

And how many more cases do you think that might be? she asked herself. Actually, the comment presented itself to her in Peter's voice. *One more case? Maybe two? Let's not forget that you're on a ticking clock, Rach.*

But for half a day or so, she'd managed to almost forget it. She'd been able to work this case without being hindered by her diagnosis. She'd had a slight headache yesterday and nothing more—and really, that could have been nothing more than the product of the intense desert heat.

They'd been driving toward the address—now just eleven miles away—when Duvall called back. Rachel answered on speaker mode so

Jack could also listen in. "So there *is* a bit of a record on our friend Brett Alvarez," she said. "Two years ago, he was charged with assault. He assaulted an intoxicated woman at a party. And this party just happened to be out in the desert, around a big bonfire."

"Well, that certainly lines up," Rachel said

"Yeah, I thought so, too. Oh, and it gets even better. While I was looking into that, I had a cop take a look at the phone records of Malorie and Valerie. Brett Alvarez's number was in both of their phones. Malorie had him saved as 'Alvy' and Valerie had him saved as 'Happy Man.'"

"That's…incriminating."

"I'll say. How much further do you have before you arrive?"

"About ten miles. Thanks for all of this, Duvall. You've been a massive help."

"I do what I can."

They ended the call, and with this new information on Alvarez, Rachel pressed on the gas a bit harder. She pushed the car to eighty-five, the desert whipping by in a blur of oranges, tans, and blue sky.

"I feel like we're living in a crappy classic rock song," Jack joked. "Tearing down a desert highway with a grand adventure in front of us."

"I never cared for those kinds of songs," she said. "But I can get behind the adventure idea of it all, I suppose."

Jack chuckled, but Rachel meant it. While there was, of course, the immediate urgency of catching the killer before he could strike again, it was always the hunt itself that had pushed Rachel. And yes, there was a certain degree of adventure to it. It boiled down to her childhood love of solving puzzles, often overly complex ones that left most of her friends and classmates scratching their heads. Because really, what was a murder case other than a real-life puzzle?

With her eyes on the unwinding road ahead, she felt this current puzzle finally starting to come together, with the biggest piece they had yet to find waiting just a few miles ahead.

***

Brett Alvarez's apartment was located in what Rachel assumed was the back corner of Foxham. It was set within a large brick building that looked as if it had not been maintained in many years. The brick, originally dark red, was brutally faded to something much lighter from years of unprotected sun exposure. The building itself would have looked like a generic building found in the downtown area of any small town—featureless and bland, broken apart only by doors and a few windows. The only feature that gave the impression there were residences were small, wooden steps and tiny porches sitting in front of each of the five doors along the building's face. One of the porches had a small charcoal grill sitting beside it; another, a plastic chair.

Rachel parked her car beside the only two vehicles in the gravel patch that served as a parking lot. One was a beat-up Chevy truck with a busted taillight, and the other was an old Cavalier that looked as old as Rachel.

"One thing is for sure," Jack said as they stepped out and approached Alvarez's door. "If Alvarez is indeed selling drugs, the drug economy sucks around here.

Jack knocked on the door as Rachel stepped up onto the small porch and looked around. A few blocks behind them, the small center of Foxham sat in the sun. A few cars meandered around here and there, but the place looked dead for the most part. The only noise she could hear at all was the blaring of a television from one of the neighboring apartments.

Ten seconds passed, then twenty. Jack hammered on the door again, with much more force this time. "Brett Alvarez," he hollered. "You in there?"

Again, they waited. Rachel stepped up to the door, placing her ear within a few inches of it. She could hear nothing coming from inside, no footsteps, no movement, no music, or the sounds of a television.

When it was clear Alvarez either wasn't home or *was* home and choosing not to answer the door, Jack shrugged. "What do you say, Gift? Do we have enough speculation against him for me to kick down the door? Even if he's not home, we could maybe find some stuff to help nail him."

Rachel thought it over. They didn't have nearly enough evidence to promote the idea that Alvarez was the murderer. But they had a pretty tall mountain of evidence to back up the theory that Alvarez was planning secret raves and parties in the desert and selling drugs. The real kicker, though, was that his name was on the phones of all three of the victims. Rachel figured she and Jack would get their hands slapped for busting the door down, but she was willing to accept that.

She nearly gave her vocal agreement but closed her mouth when a car came turning into the small driveway. It was a black BMW, slightly coated in desert dust. The driver turned in slowly, looking down at his phone. When the gravel started to crunch under his tires, he looked up in order to guide the car to a parking spot. Yet when he saw the two agents standing by the door immediately to left of the spot he was angling for, he brought the car to a sudden halt.

He looked directly at them for about two seconds. Rachel then saw him reaching for the gear shift lever by the steering wheel. Even before he shifted into reverse, Rachel knew this was their guy—that this was Brett Alvarez, arriving home and spooked to find two people at his door. Two people that were dressed in a manner a little too close to what everyone thought federal agents dressed in.

"That's him," Rachel said. "Get in the car, Jack."

She took a single step forward and the driver—presumably Alvarez—threw the BMW into reverse. Gravel crunched and spun up, pinging against the underside of the car. There was not any question among Rachel or Jack; she slipped behind the wheel of their own car while Jack got into the passenger side.

"You good with this?" Jack asked as she started the car.

She smirked, adrenaline slamming hard against her heart. "Oh yeah. Buckle up."

She backed out of the lot quickly, cutting hard to the right into the cloud of gray dust the BMW had kicked up. By the time she sped out of the cloud and the gravel driveway, she saw that the BMW was already a good distance away. It had blasted ahead, in the direction of what Rachel had been thinking of as the center of Foxham.

"What the hell is this idiot thinking?" Jack said. "Is he really just going to try to get into a high-speed car chase in a small town in the middle of the desert?"

"He knows the town a lot better than we do," Rachel noted. "Call Duvall, would you? Tell her to alert the Foxham PD about the situation. If we get a few more cars on this, he's screwed."

Jack nodded and did as she asked while Rachel pressed harder on the gas. She saw the BMW take a hard right turn up ahead. No turn signal, and barely slowing. It missed slamming into a truck at the intersection by less than a foot or so.

As Rachel made her way to that same turn, the truck now having turned right and pulling away from the scene, she heard Jack giving the report to Duvall. She scanned the road ahead, a simple two-lane that arrowed between a small row of businesses. The BMW was two blocks further ahead, already taking another turn. Small town and wide-open spaces or not, she feared that another turn like that, and the little bastard might slip right away from her.

Fortunately, the streets weren't very busy. She saw only two other moving cars and they were further ahead, stopped at a red light. She

91

rocketed the car forward, pushing fifty through an intersection and then turning right to follow the BMW. She saw him instantly. He'd remained on a straight course, currently blasting around a car and into the oncoming lane.

"He's heading for the highway," Jack said. He was still on the phone, apparently speaking to both Rachel *and* Duvall. Rachel had worried about this, too. If he made it to the highway, things would be more tense. It would be best for everyone if she could catch up to him here, nab him before he made a real scene.

With an angry scowl on her face Rachel stamped down on the accelerator. The engine revved and the car bucked forward. She was doing eighty by the time she came to the next intersection, slamming down on the horn to alert the three cars that were stopped there and waiting for the light to turn. She sensed Jack stiffening in the seat beside her, back pressed into the seat. She didn't dare take her eyes off of the road, but she could easily imagine a nervous smile on his face.

The BMW took a very sudden left-hand turn just as Jack got off the phone. Rachel was close enough to the car now that she could see the outline of Alvarez's head protruding over the back of the driver's seat. She slowed a bit and took the same turn. She took it fast and wide, the tires squealing and slightly bumping against the curb of sidewalk on the passenger side. By the time she cleared the turn and was once again straightened out, she saw just how close the car was. There were only four or five car lengths between them now. If they continued at this pace for the next mile and a half or so—before Foxham emptied back out into the desert highway, she thought she may even be able to get in front of him and cut him off. The call to the police may have been a little preemptive after all. She urged the car to go faster, still blaring the horn as a sign of warning and—

Pain, brutally sharp and instant, flared through her head.

For a moment, she thought Alvarez had fired a gun at them and the bullet had taken her in the head. But no...there had been no blast or cracking of the windshield.

And then there was a blinding flash of light. It seemed to come at her like a missile—starting as a bright pinpoint in the distance and then it was right there, directly in front of her, inside the car and swallowing her whole world. The pain seemed to suck it in, luring it right into her head.

She cried out in surprise and pain, forgetting for just a moment that she was behind the wheel of a car.

"Rachel!"

It was Jack, from some other place, some other world on the other side of that white light. Rachel winced and forced herself to feel the steering wheel in her hands, the pedals at her feet. The light dissipated quickly, just in time for her to see that the car was about to hit the curb on the opposite side of the road.

She slammed on the brakes. The car still struck the curb and hopped it, but there were thankfully no pedestrians. She stared out at the street, the world tilted and fuzzy.

Alvarez...shit. He's gone.

"Jack...switch with me. Take the wheel." She fumbled for the door handle, eager to get out.

"Rachel, wait. Are you okay? What was that?"

'Just a headache. Just a bad...a bad—"

"That's bullshit, Rachel. Just...just hold on, okay?"

She heard him get out of the car and then he was on her side, opening the door for her and helping her out. Her vision crew clearer and clearer by the moment. She felt the street under her shoes, felt her knees bending as Jack helped her against the building directly beside them and then lowered her to the ground. She sat there for a moment as Jack hunkered down beside her.

"What was that, Rachel?"

"I don't know."

"Don't lie to me."

"Jack...can we just get back to Alvarez?"

"There are local cops on his tail right now. Don't you hear the sirens?"

She took a moment to close her mouth, to calm her breath. When she focused, she *could* hear the sirens. They were close, and heading away from them, in the same direction as the speeding BMW.

"Is it the tumor?" Jack asked.

She didn't want to answer him. She didn't want to give him one more thing to worry about, one more reason to baby her.

"Yeah, I think so," she finally said.

"What do you need right now?"

She felt anger rising up in her but swallowed it down, trying to remind herself that he was only worried about her He cared for her and wanted to make sure she was okay. She was the priority to him in this moment; Alvarez and the case was second. And honestly, she wasn't sure how to feel about that.

"Honestly, nothing," she said. "Those little episodes, they come and go. My head is still hurting, but it's fading. Based on past experiences, it'll be gone within fifteen minutes or so."

"You're not lying?"

"No," she said, getting to ger feet. The earth was stable again and her vision was back. No fuzziness, no bright, sudden flashes of light. "Now get behind the wheel. Let's see what we can do to help."

"Fine," he said, walking to the driver's side door. It was still open from her getting out, dinging incessantly. "But you and I...we need to talk about this soon, Rachel. I hate to point out the obvious. You were flying—and rightfully so—but you know we could have—"

"We could have died," she snapped. "Yes, I know. I was the one behind the wheel. I know."

With an immense weight of anger, guilt, and fear raining down on her, she stormed over to the passenger side. It was a disarming anger because she wasn't clear on who she was mad at: herself, Jack for being too protective, or the killer that continued to elude them on this case. Maybe a bit of all three.

As she buckled in, the thrumming in her head continued but she tried not to look too uncomfortable in front of Jack. He got behind the wheel, backed the car off of the sidewalk, and started in the direction of the highway.

A tense silence fell between them and neither of them spoke again until they were back on the highway, approaching the swirling lights of police car bubbles. Three patrol cars were on the side of the road, with a black BMW pinned between them. Jack pulled up behind the last of the police cars just as Brett Alvarez was pushed against the side of his BMW and handcuffed.

CHAPTER NINETEEN

The interior of the Foxham police station was more quaint and welcoming than Rachel had been expecting. Being a small town, it was an equally small building. But it was set up more like a casual office than most police stations Rachel had ever seen. The bullpen was like a well-structured set of cubicles and the east and west walls were occupied with sets of offices that looked overly tidy. It was something of a blessing, actually; the well-ordered environment made her headache a bit more bearable.

Rachel and Jack walked by all of this, though. One of the cops that made the arrest on Brett Alvarez led them to the back of the primary room where a swinging door with frosted glass in its center opened onto a brightly lit hallway. It was a short hallway with two holding cells at the far end and two interrogation rooms on the right side.

They entered the hallway just as Alvarez was led into the first interrogation room. He was complaining about not being treated fairly, that his arrest was unjust. And he was doing so with a high, pitchy voice that was filled with panic. It was the voice of a man that knew what was coming, having already been arrested in the past for his assault charge.

When Alvarez was placed in a chair behind a small laminate table, the three cops that had worked on the chase and arrest looked to Rachel and Jack. Two of them looked eager to help while the other, a younger officer, seemed reluctant—like he wanted a piece of whatever action was to come.

"You two need anything else out of us?" the elder officer asked.

"No thanks," Rachel said. "But you guys did a fantastic job Thanks so much for the assist."

The older officer gave her a nod of gratitude and led the other two out. When they were gone, Jack softly closed the door behind them. There were two other chairs in the room, one on their side of the table and another in the corner. Jack grabbed the one in the corner and carried it over to the table. Together, he and Rachel sat down across from Brett Alvarez.

"Mr. Alvarez," Jack said, "do you have any guesses as to why we may have been knocking on your door today?"

"No. Not at all." His voice was still high-pitched and fearful, but the answer was fast and snappy.

"No?" Rachel asked. "Then why did you make a point to pull out and drive away from us very quickly?"

He had no answer for this. She could see his eyes wandering, the gears turning in his head. He was trying to come up with a believable lie, and Rachel wasn't about to even entertain it.

"If you lie to us, it's really going to piss me off," Rachel said. "So rather than you wasting our time and making things even harder for yourself, I'll just *tell* you why were at your door. Does that sound good?"

Alvarez looked aghast at this. The worried look on his face made him look like a troubled teen. He looked quite young as it was, anyway. He had brown hair that looked to have had frosted tips at one time. He had a handsome face that was accentuated by deep, brown eyes. While it felt a bit stereotypical, he *did* have the look of a young man that might know a thing or two about seducing women at parties.

"Sure," he said, his voice now little more than a whisper.

"We're federal agents from the East Coast, and we were called out here to look into a series of murders. Currently, we have three dead women, killed in a very specific and gruesome fashion. There are currently two solid links between all three of them: all three of them used psychedelic drugs in some capacity, and they all had your phone number in their phones."

She saw the realization settle in over his face. There was fear at first and then an odd sort of relief. "Oh. I mean…three women, dead? I don't…my number?"

"Yes," she said.

"Not to sound like an ass, but lots of people in this area have my number."

"Are they all part of the chain that is used to send invites to your little desert raves?" Jack asked.

"Yeah. So really, those two connections between them aren't all that weird, right? I mean, there are at least one hundred people on that chain. And I'd say over half of them are women."

"And now three of them are dead," Rachel said. "And I'd really like to know why."

The fear came rushing back into Alvarez's eyes. "Wait…you think I have something to do with it?"

"We think you had *at least* the drugs to do with it, yes," Rachel said. "And we figure if they're on your little chain, you probably know them. Their names are Malorie Osborne, Valerie Mitcham, and Maria Herrera."

"Hold on. First of all, I do *not* sell drugs. I don't even *do* drugs anymore. Secondly, I don't know the names of everyone on that text chain. Honestly, I probably don't even know more than half of them."

"So what's your part in these raves?" Rachel asked.

"Literally just planning them. Finding the spot, hiring a dj of sorts. Hell, I even try to always have at least two or three people there that I *know* aren't going to be doing drugs so they can offer rides to people that get blitzed."

"So there *are* drugs at these things?" Jack asked.

"Yeah. But I don't supply them."

"But you don't try to keep them out either, right?"

"No," he admitted. "Like it or not, it's just part of the culture. And by the way, you keep saying *rave*. It's not even that, really. It's not that repetitive techno garbage with the garbage beats and hooks. This is more of a trance sort of thing. The music is a huge part of it, sure. There's a whole psychedelic movement. And I don't go all Nazi on the drugs there because they're all harmless."

"In your opinion," Rachel pointed out.

"Yes, in my opinion. And that right there…*that* mindset is why I tried to run from you. I think deep down I've been expecting it for a while now. I'm the guy that throws these raves where there's drugs and maybe a small orgy here and there from time to time. I sort of create the atmosphere and let the drug use happen. I figured someone would try to bust me eventually."

"Yeah, I still don't buy it," Jack said. "You were hauling ass. You were doing everything you could to get away from us."

"I'm clean, man. Search my car, my apartment, whatever you need."

It was a brazen statement and it made Rachel wonder if he might be actually telling the truth. "Anyone ever die at one of your get-togethers?" Rachel asked.

"No. Sometimes people will pass out or get a little sick to the stomach from some of the drugs—mushrooms mostly. But no one has ever died."

"Has anyone gone wandering off into the desert?"

"I don't know. I can't keep up with everyone that comes. I'm sure there have been a few that have wandered off for a quickie or alone time or something. I mean, if they come and then wander off and do their own thing, how the hell am I supposed to be responsible for that?"

The uncaring attitude rubbed Rachel the wrong way. For a moment, she thought she felt her headache coming back. And now that she was sitting still, looking directly at Alvarez, she also sensed that the vision in her right eye was sort of blurry.

"Tell me this," Rachel said. "Do the women that come out to these things know about your record? Do they know about your assault charge?"

"No."

Jack sat forward and Rachel could already tell he was uncomfortable with how quickly she was losing her temper. "Mr. Alvarez, do you keep any sort of log of who shows up at these parties?"

"No, I just send out the invites."

"And when they start, do you ty to meet and greet a lot of those that arrive?"

"Not really. I mostly hang with the dj." He seemed to hesitate before he continued but decided it might be worth it to be as honest as possible, apparently. "Most nights, I do end up leaving with one of the women that show up. But that's it."

"And those three names we gave you...none of those sound familiar?"

Alvarez shook his head. "I'm sorry, man. No. Look...I'm sorry as hell that three women have died, but I don't see why I'm being eyed for this. I just had their numbers because they were part of the chain I swear, man. Look at anything I have! I'm clean."

Rachel hated that she was starting to believe him. Still, there was one last thing that started to nag at her. "Are you a religious man by any chance?"

"No. I mean, I was raised in the church but stopped going pretty much after I moved out of my parents' house."

"No interest in theology or religious symbols?"

"Not at all," he said, furrowing his brow in confusion.

Just based on his reaction, this was another area where Rachel was inclined to believe him. And if that was the case, she wasn't sure how someone with no fervor of religion would be driven to pose their victims in a Christ-like pose with their hearts removed.

"And what about last night? Do you have proof of your whereabouts for most of the night?"

"There are a few people that can back me up, yeah. And if you can give me my phone, I should have plenty of video evidence, too."

If all of this was truthful, he was as good as free. Rachel once again felt the case slipping further away.

"Thank you," she said briskly. She got up, triggered by something she'd just said. *No interest in theology or religious symbols?...*

She walked back out into the brightly lit hallway, walking aimlessly back toward the holding cells. Both were empty. Jack came out seconds later and joined her.

"You okay?" he asked.

"I think so. I was—"

"Is it your head?"

"No," she said, doing her best to keep the irritation out of her voice. "But I just had a thought. The staging of the bodies...I don't know if we're focusing on that enough. It's definitely ritualistic. But I wonder if it's not just some random, strange staging the killer is doing on his own—some made up gesture or symbol. What if he's copying some other sort of ritual? And even now, as I say it all out loud, I think about the removal of the hearts. Surely there's some sort of ritual practice somewhere throughout history that lines up with what the killer is doing."

"It's a good thought for sure. But I don't know that we have the time to be researching every messed-up sort of sacrifice known in recorded history."

"Maybe we can get a head start."

Rachel grabbed her phone from her pocket and once again called Duvall. Honestly, relying on Duvall was starting to feel like a crutch but it just made sense to use every tool at their disposal—especially if it was a third agent that had a tendency to quickly get things done. As the phone started ringing, Rachel experienced another brief flare of pain in her head. Her right eye remained a bit fuzzy, almost as if a filter was placed in front of her eye for a moment and quickly yanked away, only to come again seconds later.

"This is Duvall," came an eventual answer in Rachel's ear.

"Duvall, it's Agent Gift. Listen, you're familiar with the area, right?"

"A little too much, honestly. What do you need?"

"I'm wondering if your field office has anyone around Albuquerque that might serve as a resource of sorts when it comes to ritualistic murders or cult activity."

"I'm not too sure, actually. I know there's a guy at a non-profit that we use sometimes for Native American rights and folklore, but that's not what you're looking for. You could—oh! Oh, you know what? Yes. There's a guy in Santa Fe, a professor at the community college. A colleague of mine was emailing back and forth with him at some point last year when we thought there was some weird religious group leaving dead chickens on the porches of police officers' homes. I'm pretty sure he has a background in rituals, shaman-type magic, and things like that."

"Is there any way you can send me his information?"

"For sure. Actually, I'm headed your way right now—straight to the Foxham PD to coordinate with the cops on the arrest they just made. I'll have it for you by the time I get there. Say twenty minutes?"

"That would be great. You're a rock star, Duvall."

"You can't see it, but I'm playing air guitar as we speak. See you soon."

Rachel ended the call, deep in thought. While she wasn't quite ready to release Brett Alvarez just yet, it was quite clear that he wasn't the killer. And even if he was, they were a very long way away from having enough evidence to convict him.

"Duvall's on her way," Rachel said. "I wonder...when she gets here, do you want to work with her to take Alvarez up on his offer to search everything he has? Apartment, car, clothes, whatever."

"Sure. But what about you?"

"If all goes well, I'll be taking a crash course in ritual practices with a guy out of Santa Fe."

"Fun stuff. And I'm going to ask one last time: you're sure you're okay?"

She gave him a smirk that was only partly genuine. "And this is the last time I'll answer. It was sudden and unexpected and a little scary. But for right now, yes. I'm fine."

"Okay, but your driving privileges are hereby suspended. You want the keys, you'll have to fight me for them."

"That's fair enough. Now, if you'll excuse me, I'm going to find some coffee."

She took her leave, with Jack still hanging out by the holding cell. And while Rachel did indeed want a cup of coffee, she had another reason for stepping away from Jack. Although she knew there was no way he could know it, her eye continued to blur in and out of focus and the guilt of lying to him about it was much less overwhelming when she wasn't standing directly beside him.

CHAPTER TWENTY

Rachel was starting to understand that Agent Duvall either had the respect of just about everyone within a one-hundred-mile radius, or she bullied her way into getting what she wanted *when* she wanted it. Whichever might be the case, Duvall had made sure Rachel had access to the professor from Santa Fe as soon as possible. That's how Rachel ended up sitting in the vacant interrogation room with a laptop on the table in front of her, watching a FaceTime screen connect to Professor Kele Paddock just fifteen minutes after Jack and Duvall had left to search Brett Alvarez's apartment and car.

The call connected and Rachel found herself looking at a man of Native American descent. Professor Paddock looked to be in his late fifties or early sixties, his shoulder-length hair gone mostly gray. He wore a pair of small bifocals and a subtle yet attractive beaded necklace around his thin neck.

"Professor Paddock, thank you so much for taking my call," Rachel said. "I promise I won't keep you very long."

"I'm glad to help," Paddock said in a soft-spoken voice. "I have forty minutes before my next class begins, so you're welcome to however much of that time you'd like. Agent Duvall tells me there have been three murders in the desert that may have some sort of ritualistic roots, is that right?"

"That's how it seems," Rachel said. "But I want to know for sure before we just start assuming or dismissing things."

"What characteristics of the murders make you lean toward ritual practices?"

"Well, the women have all been found in the desert, all displayed on rocks that are protruding from the ground. It seems the killer has made an attempt to keep the bodies from touching the ground. The throats are all slit, and the hearts have been removed. All three women have been nude, situated to look almost as if they've been crucified. There's something about the way the bodies are situated that makes you instantly think of Christ on the cross, right down to the circular markings of blood by each hand. But it's the hearts being removed that keeps tripping me up. They aren't being removed with brutal strength or a sloppy approach. It seems like the killer has been very careful."

Paddock thought this over for a moment, nodding. "You say it seems the killer is being careful with how the hearts are removed. Would you go so far as to say he's removed the hearts with a show of something close to respect?"

"Yes, I think it could be described like that."

"And were the bodies…um, were they violated sexually?"

"No. They were also right around the same age."

"By any chance were they in their early twenties, give or take a few years? In decent shape?"

Rachel got chill bumps at the guess. She grinned nervously. "That's exactly right. I'm guessing it sounds familiar to you?"

"It does, yes. The Christ-like pose throws me off a bit, but the important thing here is that the arms were splayed. Spread open as if in flight almost?"

Rachel saw each of the victims in her mind, bare chests to the sky. She supposed the outstretched arms *could* be mimicking wings opened for flight. "Yes, I'd say that's a fitting description."

"What you're describing is indicative of an ancient Aztec ritual— one that required human sacrifice. These sacrifices were often done in large groups, as many as fifty women at a time. And it was always younger women, just out of their developing years but also before any true sort of age set in. The most beautiful and most skilled or athletic would be taken to altars as sacrifices. Their hearts would be removed as an offering to one of many gods, but it was usually the Sun God."

It was chilling to hear, especially after Professor Paddock had been able to guess the age and appearance of the victims. It all made a sick sort of sense now, but it did nothing to help her feel better about the case.

"And the Sun God…what was he worshipped for?"

"The Sun God is the giver of life. They praised and worshipped the sun for all of their good fortunes and relied on those practices for longevity and a healthy life."

She considered this, butting it against one very alarming fact Paddock had told her: *these sacrifices were often done in large groups, as many as fifty women at a time.*

Their killer didn't honestly intend to kill that many, did he? Or maybe it *was* a cult. Maybe with a jointed effort, multiple men believed it might be possible.

"Professor, would you happen to know if any cults in the area have an interest in this sort of ritual sacrifice?"

Paddock sighed and ran a hand through his long, thinning hair. "None that I know of. Of course, that might mean nothing at all. Smaller sects can sort of stay hidden easily out in the desert. The only group I can think of around your area that would be at all involved with any sort of ritual practices would be a small group of Satanists. But I don't see their ideologies lining up with the sort of grisly practices you're mentioning."

She felt a brief stirring of promise but dashed it away at once. She had nearly fallen into accepting the stereotype that Satanists were evil animal-sacrificing monsters. And while she knew there was a very small percentage that *did* take it to those extremes, she also knew that actual human sacrifice was pretty much unheard of.

"Have you ever had any interactions with this group?"

"Once," Paddock said. "A member of their group was in my Primitive Cultures class. I'm not going to say anything for certain, but I doubt this specific group has done anything more than light some red candles and *maybe* kill a chicken or two."

"So…ancient Aztec, huh?"

"Yes. What you've described to me sounds almost identical. If you'll give me your email address or cell number, I can send you a few illustrations."

At that same time, someone knocked on the door. It opened just a fraction and she saw the older cop that had arrested Brett Alvarez poke his head in. Rachel waved him in as she recited her email address to Paddock.

"Give me about five or ten minutes," Paddock said. "I'll send you something."

"That would be great. Thanks again for your time, Professor."

"Hey, I just hoped I was of some help. Good luck on the case, agent."

With that, they ended the call. Rachel closed the lid of the borrowed laptop and looked at the policeman. "What's up?"

"I thought you'd want to know that after you and your partner left Alvarez alone, we went in to see if we could get some of the names of people he *did* remember from some of his raves. We also asked about the nights of the murders, like where he was and all of that."

"Oh, they aren't raves," Rachel pointed out. "Careful, he's touchy about that."

"That's right. I noticed that. But. He did give us his phone, right out of his pocket. And as we were looking, he got this look on his face, this excited sort of thing. Told us that he could prove he was pretty much in the clear."

Having said that, the officer set a phone on the table in front of her. It was unlocked, the screen showing a video. The play icon was in the center of the screen, the video waiting to be played.

"This was recorded last night between eleven at night and five in the morning."

She played the video and saw Alvarez standing behind a very small table with another man. The man was clearly a dj, swaying behind a computer set up with a massive pair of headphones over his ears. Trance-like electronic music was playing and a few strobe lights were flashing, revealing the open expanse of the desert behind them. Here and there, an arm or the top of a head came into view, as the camera was set up high, likely on a portable speaker, Rachel assumed. She checked the length of the video and saw that there was six more minutes remaining.

"We checked through them all. There are fourteen videos from last night. Some are just four or five minutes, and there are a few on there that are nearly half an hour. And they pretty much take up the entire night. Sure, he could have dipped out between some of them, but I think it tells a pretty good story for us."

Rachel stopped the first video and went to the gallery. The officer was right; all of the videos showed Alvarez with the dj. Some of them were almost like tutorials for how to run the dj's set-up, as Alvarez filmed it. Apparently, he was trying to learn how to run the system. Two other videos showed that this was very much the case, while Alvarez manned the station while the hired dj walked off to the side to have a drink.

"Well, damn."

"Sorry, Agent Grace."

"It's fine. Thank *you* for taking the initiative." She stared at the collection of videos for a moment, curious. "How much manpower could the PD offer for a minimal task at the moment?"

"Not sure. We'd have to check in with the Sheriff, but I'd imagine maybe three or four. Why?"

"I can't help but wonder if we could catch shots of the victim on these videos—of Maria Herrera. Maybe even a shot of her interacting with the killer."

The cop pointed at her in a sort of a-ha gesture, as if they'd just won a round of Pictionary. "Yeah. Let me get some guys on that."

"Thanks," she said. "If you find anything or need an assist, get in touch with Agent Duvall and we'll see what we can do."

The cop seemed happy enough to have an important assignment when Rachel left the room. She paused by the interrogation room that still held Alvarez but figured even if he was one hundred percent cleared, he'd likely be there for a few more hours. Right now, she wanted to get out of the station. As ominous as that wide-open desert was, she wanted to be outside. The headache was still lurking, and she had an internal assurance that fresh air would somehow help.

She left the building and walked slowly to the car she and Jack had been using. She breathed in the humid air and looked up the that perfect blue sky. Looking at the sky, the slight blur to her right eye wasn't as noticeable. And when she looked away from it to the front of the police station, she thought it was nearly back to normal.

Although she knew it would royally piss Jack off, she got back behind the wheel of the car. She figured she could meet Jack and Duvall back over at Alvarez's apartment. She reached for the ignition and found it empty.

Instead, there was a small scrap of paper—a thin, grimy sort, like from a receipt. It had been rolled up tightly and gingerly placed in the ignition as far as it would go. She unrolled it and found a message. She read it, both laughing and letting out her favorite four-letter word.

The letter read: *You weren't thinking of trying to drive, were you? Hope not, because I got the keys.*

"Jack, you're the worst," she said with a smile.

With that, she headed back inside. First, she thought she'd get some Ibuprofen for the ghost of her headache. And then maybe she'd pitch in and help with scouring the footage from Alvarez's phone. Menial and repetitive or not, it felt like a necessary step in getting closer to their killer.

CHAPTER TWENTY ONE

Now that he was able to see her in person, he realized that he'd seen her before. At one of the parties out in the desert. He wasn't sure how he'd overlooked her. She wasn't what most people would consider beautiful, but she was attractive. She had nice legs and carried herself with the sort of confidence that didn't come off as cocky. Brown hair and, from what he could tell, hazel eyes.

It was hard to be sure of the eye color because he had yet to get that close to her.

He'd been following her at a distance for the last two hours. Her shift at Liminal Coffee House had ended at two in the afternoon. Once she'd left there, taking her barista apron off and tossing it into her car, she'd spritzed on some perfume and walked three blocks to meet up with a friend. The pair had then walked another block and stopped at a bar. He'd entered a few minutes behind them and spotted them sitting at the bar, sipping on beers. He'd taken a seat in the small diner area, totally unnoticed by the girls as he ate nachos and drank a soda.

He'd finished up before they did, as they'd ordered another round. While he waited for them to come out, he crossed the street and sat on a bench in front of a mobile phone store. He pretended to scroll around on his phone until the girls came out. He watched them hug and then part ways. He waited about thirty seconds and started following his target again.

After another block or so back in the direction of her car, she stopped at a music store called Classic Cuts—a pretty stupid name for a music store in his opinion. He again waited another minute or so before also walking in. The place was pretty busy for nearly four in the afternoon, so he again went mostly unseen.

And that's how he'd come to be standing in front of the Metal section, casting glances her way and trying to determine the color of her eyes. She was standing over near the Folk Rock section, looking at the back of a Mount Eerie record. When she set the record back in the stacks, she almost caught him looking at her. He narrowly avoided the eye contact by picking up the first record in front of him. Gojira. What the hell kind of a name was that?

He then went ahead and assumed the role of a basic customer. He kept the record in his hand and wandered over to the aisle she was standing in. He stopped shy of Folk Rock and instead started flipping through the Ambient section. To his surprise, the girl—named Ashlyn Myers, he knew—moved past him, their backs nearly touching.

"Sorry," she said. "Excuse me."

He looked up and met her eyes. He'd been right. They were hazel. "No problem," he said. And then, as if hit by a sudden stroke of genius, he kept talking. It was risky, but he just went with it. It just felt right.

"Hey…are you…sorry. I know it sounds like a bad pick-up line, but I swear I've seen you before. Recently, too."

She eyed him oddly, though not with suspicion. "Yeah?" she asked skeptically.

"Yeah. Did I…did I run into you at the Lost Heroes show last week?" He had no idea who Lost Heroes were or if they were even a real group at all. He'd heard some stoner talking about them at one of the more recent parties he'd been to out in the desert.

"No…"

"Huh. Okay." He shrugged as if it were no big deal. "Sorry."

"It's okay."

She took a single step away and he continued to play the part. "Oh! Oh, I got it." He leaned a bit closer, as if about to reveal a secret. "Do you go to the desert raves every now and then?"

She smiled and good God, it nearly killed him. Maybe she *was* beautiful after all. "Maybe," she said.

"That's where! I knew I'd seen you before."

"When's the last one you went to?" Ashlyn asked. She was smiling at him now, tucking a loose strand of that brown hair behind her left ear.

"Last night. Before that, it's been about a week, I guess."

"So you saw me, and remembered me without talking to me?" she asked. "I'm not sure how to feel about that."

"Yikes," he said, doing his best to play it off. "Yeah, I guess that does come off as creepy, huh?"

"Some girls may be flattered," she said. "Me…well, I don't know yet."

"Do you go to all of them?"

"Not really. I'm not a big fan of the music—just the scene, you know?"

"Eh, it's not so bad." This was a lie. He fucking hated that psychedelic bleep-boop crap they listened to at the desert raves. "You going to the next one?"

"I might," she said, smiling in a way that was *almost* flirting, but not quite. "Depends on when it is. And…maybe depends on who else might be there."

The smile she gave him was pretty much a *yes*, though—so long as he was going to be there.

"Good," he said. "Maybe I'll see you there."

"If I decide to go…yeah, I hope you will."

"In that case, I really think you should go to the next one."

It had been a while since he'd actually spoken with a woman in this way. He knew it wasn't anything promising but it felt like progress. If he were looking for a woman to date or just for a night of fun, this might be a good start. He just wasn't sure anymore.

Of course, a night of fun was the last thing on his mind. He was thinking of the jar Ashlyn's heart would be going in.

Ashlyn said nothing else. She let him take in her smile for another second before turning away. He watched her head to the counter to pay for two records and then turned his attention back to the stacks. He was feeling so good about what had just happened that he stopped playing a part and walked over to the Punk section. He grabbed up a Black Flag import he'd wanted since he was nineteen and didn't even mind the steep price when he checked out.

He was far too excited.

She hadn't given him a *yes,* but he had a good feeling.

For all he knew, Ashlyn might be the final one, the one that finished the ritual.

He thought of what it would be like to be done—to never fear death again.

Soon Ashlyn's heart would be with the others, and it would join in their singing.

CHAPTER TWENTY TWO

The videos on Alvarez's phone were put on the station's internal server, giving Rachel easy access to them from the same laptop she'd used to contact Professor Paddock. Rachel had watched only two so far, taking her time to go through them with painstaking attention. So far, though, the phone camera had picked up only one person that was not Brett Alvarez or the dj—a man wearing only a pair of baggy shorts, clearly high on something and dancing to the music in a way that reminded Rachel of an inchworm.

To her right, her phone showed her one of the two pictures Professor Paddock had sent her. It was a pen-and-ink drawing of the ritual he had described. From the looks of it, the artists had drawn the ritual taking place in a small coliseum-style area. Several people looked on, all naked except for a small loin cloth. In the center of the picture, two men held a nude woman down on a stone slab while her heart was cut out. Her arms were stretched out as if she were trying to fly, held down on either side by the men. Her legs had been tied to the slab, also stretched out.

She glanced at it as the second video ended. It displayed the crime scenes perfectly, the only slight difference being the positioning of the feet. Aztec. Deserts. Drugs and raves. What the hell was the connection here?

She was about to start on her third video when her cellphone rang. She was fully expecting it to be Jack or Duvall, calling with findings (or lack thereof) from their search of Alvarez's apartment. Instead, it turned out to be Shirley Baxter, the county coroner.

She answered the call and stood up from the same table she'd been using in the free interrogation room, happy to be looking away from the laptop screen. "This is Agent Gift."

"Agent Gift, it's Shirley Baxter. I've got some very preliminary findings from Maria Herrera's bloodwork, and I thought you might want to know that she also had traces of a hallucinogenic drug in her system. It wasn't a very strong one, but it's there. And again, it was sort of a rushed job. It may appear stronger in the more precise tests."

"What drug, exactly?" Even if it *was* just preliminary and nothing official yet, it was. a huge break. Rachel couldn't help but feel a little glimmer of hope.

"Looks like peyote based on what I've seen in some drug work in the past."

"Peyote?" Rachel asked, a bit confused. "Slightly different from what was found in the other two."

"True. But peyote also slips into popular culture with certain groups. I've seen it a few times. I'm sure you'll find it in current arrest records within the area, too."

"Would you happen to know if it's popular with rave crowds?"

"Sorry, I don't know for sure. But at the end of the day, peyote *does* offer some of the same experiences those other rave drugs do. Used correctly, there are some circles around here that use it as medicine. But it can also cause some pretty intense hallucinations."

"Thanks, Dr. Baxter. This actually helps a lot."

"Good. Now if you could find the guy that's doing this, I'd appreciate it. I'm already tired of looking at pretty young girls that have had their hearts ripped out."

"I'll do my best," she said, ending the call.

She closed the laptop lid and exited the interrogation room. As she walked back to the small and very clean bullpen, she could hear a cop speaking to Alvarez in the first interrogation room. She found a small waiting area to the right of the bullpen, just as immaculate and clean as the rest of the place. She sat down in a surprisingly comfortable chair and let her mind wander as she looked out to the mostly empty parking lot.

Three victims, all of whom had a hallucinogenic drug in their system. Three victims of the same age that had been lured into the desert. And while there was no guaranteed link between the three women and the desert raves, their possession of Alvarez's number seemed to point to the idea pretty hard.

Another thing occurred to her in that moment, something she was a bit embarrassed that she'd not touched on yet. If Maria had plans with Robin, then why was she high as a kite in the desert on the same night? Robin had told them she didn't think Maria did many drugs, so maybe Maria was keeping the drug use—and a much heavier involvement in this desert rave scene—a secret. So maybe Maria had planned to blow Robin off for some reason. But why? And whatever the reason was, could it be relevant to the case?

Rachel started to create a list in her head of things they could start looking into. Was there maybe some obscure Aztec link between them? Did the killer have a link to deadly Aztec practices and, if so, could they find him by searching through police records?

She also wondered *why* the man would kill in such a way. Was it a tribute to some modern-day form of the Sun God Paddock had mentioned? Or maybe they were dealing with a man that was fueled by delusions, thinking that killing these women may please an actual Sun God to the point where he was granted eternal life. That was, of course, if the killer was as well versed in Aztec legends as Paddock was.

There was also a very simple approach underpinning it all. Actually, there could even be two, and one of them was still sitting in an interrogation room just thirty feet away. She thought about this as she watched a black sedan pull into the parking lot. Duvall was behind the wheel, with Jack in the passenger seat. They were chatting about something, and she could see Jack laughing as they parked just off to the side of the window. Rachel grinned wanly as she realized the two looked cute together. Not that Jack would even think such a thing. When he was in deep on a case, he usually thought of little else.

They came into the station together and spotted Rachel in the waiting area. "We found absolutely nothing," Jack said. "There were even these annoying little pamphlets in Alvarez's apartment on how to talk people down from a high. He also has some new music gear. Some of it isn't even out of the boxes yet."

"Apparently, he's studying to become a rave dj," Rachel said. She then told them about the videos that had been found on Alvarez's phone. "We've found nothing yet, but there were close to twenty videos to go through and only three other cops looking at them."

"What about Professor Paddock?" Duvall asked. "Did he help?"

"He seems to think we're dealing with something of an ancient Aztec nature." She showed them the picture that she still had up on her phone, the pen and ink drawing of the woman having her heart removed in front of several people. "Look familiar?"

"Yeah, a little too much," Duvall said.

"I don't know about you," Jack said, looking to both women, "but based on these videos on his phone and the lack of anything suspicious in his home or car, I just don't think Alvarez is our guy."

"Probably not," Rachel agreed. "But we still have him here and I think I know a few more things we can ask him before he hits the road."

"Mind if I join in this time?" Duvall asked.

"Not at all," Rachel said. "The more the merrier."

As the three of them headed back for the interrogation rooms, Rachel had already started to work out the questions she was going to ask him. She didn't think he'd be too stubborn about talking. And if he was, she may just remind him that they now had three numbers with his text threads on them. They would know when he sent another one out and maybe they would decide to just show up one night to see what they were like.

And even that gave her another idea. She was suddenly so overcome with a series of promising approaches that it was nearly enough to allow her to overlook the fact that slowly but surely, her headache was coming back.

***

Alvarez's demeanor had changed considerably since the last time Rachel and Jack had spoken to him. He looked almost confident know, a confidence edged with just a bit of anger. Even before Rachel or Jack could say a single word, Alvarez did his best to regain some of the composure he had so badly lost the last time they'd spoken.

"You two again?" he asked, barely taking the time to also register Duvall standing behind them. "I know the videos on my phone get me off the hook. And I also haven't heard about anything popping up at my place. I told you I was innocent and now you know it. So if you have any more questions for me, I think you know what you can do with them."

"Well, I certainly hope that little rant made you feel better," Jack said. "Because the fact of the matter is that if we really wanted to, we could come up with at least three other reasons to keep you here. Assisting with the distribution of narcotics, for starters."

"And believe it or not," Rachel said, "we really don't want to do that. The more time we waste on you, the less time we're out there chasing down our killer."

"This is bullshit."

"It sort of is," Rachel said. "But just a few more questions and we'll leave you alone."

Alvarez shook his head, looking to each one of them individually. "No."

A flare of anger went spiraling through Rachel and it seemed to make the blurriness in her right eye worse for a few seconds. She took a deep breath, centered herself, and calmly approached the table.

"Three women are dead, Mr. Alvarez. Three women that have attended the raves you conduct. We have strong reason to believe that the killer is either attending these raves or distributing drugs to targeted women so that he can lure them away. Either way, your raves seem to be at the center of the equation. With your help, we may be able to make sure a fourth or fifth woman does not get murdered. You just have to try to be a decent human being for a second and answer a few last questions—questions that, honestly, aren't even about you."

She saw a softening in his expression as her vision cleared a bit. The headache was still looming in her head like a rattlesnake coiled and ready to strike. She did everything she could to make sure she remained calm. When she placed her hands on the table to lean forward, it had less to do with intimidation and more to do with making sure she didn't start swaying on her feet.

"Fine," Alvarez snapped. "What are your questions?"

"We need to find the dealer that is supplying these women. That's the first thing."

"Okay…but there's no way I could know that."

"So you throw these parties," Jack said, "and you *know* there are drugs there. But you don't know *who* is bringing the drugs in?"

"I mean, I *do*. Yeah. But I have no idea which of them is giving the drugs to these women."

"Okay, so narrow it down. It's only hallucinogens," Rachel said. "And I would assume it would be someone that is there *only* to socialize, specifically with women. The music and experience itself would be secondary only."

"I'd also suggest," Duvall said from the back of the room, "that it would probably be someone that might be rather new. Someone that has just started coming to these parties. I doubt a drug dealer that might also be carrying out these ritualistic murders has been there for a long time. Too many people would recognize his face."

Rachel wasn't completely sure she agreed with this theory, but she said nothing. There was no harm in having as many ideas as possible floating around.

A small cringe crossed Alvarez's face. The man's expressions were like reading a book. Rachel figured he was likely a very bad poker player.

"What is it?" she asked.

"I think I might know the guy. Like, I don't *know* him. Not well, anyway. He started coming about two months ago. He'd have a different girl on his arm every time, but the last two or three, he hasn't.

And yeah, I've seen him handing stuff over—usually in a small bag or in a bottle, like a prescription pill bottle. But he wasn't causing any trouble. No one really ever does at my get-togethers."

"You got a name?" Rachel asked.

"Yeah, but I don't even think it's a real name. They call him Lester, but almost as if it's like a codename or nickname or something."

From the back of the room, Duvall let out a thinly whispered curse. Rachel and Jack turned back to her and saw that she was already heading for the door. "Can I speak with you guys really quick?" she asked. "Out in the hall?"

They both nodded. But Rachel hesitated for a moment. "Jack, do you mind heading out with her. I'll be out in just a few seconds."

"Sure," he said, skeptically. "You okay?"

"Yeah. Just one more thing to cover here."

He kept his eyes on her for a moment but turned to follow Duvall after a few seconds. It was one of those strange and random moments where Rachel could feel his respect for her. He didn't question why she'd chosen to stay behind; he just went with it because he trusted her judgment. He always had—which made her feel slightly guilty as the headache still coiled inside and her right eye seemed to flicker in and out of a slight blurry haze.

As soon as the door closed, Rachel turned her attention back to Alvarez. He looked relieved once again but when their eyes locked, she could tell that he was intimidated by her.

"We're going to go after this Lester character," she said. "But just in case this doesn't pan out, you're going to create a Plan B for us."

"What? What sort of Plan B?"

"You're going to have one of your parties tonight."

"But I hadn't planned on it. I mean, I have to get the dj, and it's short notice, you know?"

"I don't care. I need you to send one of those chains out. Don't alter anything you usually do. Just send it out and plan to have it tonight."

"And let me guess. You and your partner are going to show up? Just blow the whole damned thing up?"

"We're going to show up, yes, but you'll be untouched. You do this for us, and we'll come dressed in civilian clothes. The only person that will ever know we're law enforcement will be the killer—if he's there. And again, maybe it won't even come to that. Maybe we'll hit paydirt with this drug dealer."

Alvarez considered it for a moment, clearly torn. Eventually, he met her eyes again and said: "I have your word?"

"Yes. One hundred percent."

"Fine. I'll do it."

"Good. And when you have it all planned out, I need you to leave the coordinates for the sight with one of the policemen here in the station."

"Sure. Whatever."

"Get that done and I'll do everything in my power to see that you're out of here as soon as possible."

Rachel didn't wait for a response. She hurried out of the room, once again leaving Brett Alvarez alone in the interrogation room. When she was back out in the hallway, she heard voices coming from the interrogation room she'd been using as a temporary office. She followed the sound and found Jack and Duvall huddled around the laptop she'd been using.

"What have we got?" Rachel asked.

Duvall was rapidly scrolling and clicking, her eyes never leaving the screen. "The name Lester is a dead giveaway," she said. "It's a name that used to come up here and there when I first started. He was a pretty major drug dealer in Albuquerque and all surrounding areas about five years ago. A young guy, but with connections. And he specialized in hallucinogenic. It was even rumored that he was working with a few legitimate drug labs, places that are starting to use certain psychedelics in experimental trials with schizophrenic patients. He did some jailtime after he was busted on a variety of drug charges and attempted rape of a seventeen-year-old girl. His sentence was minimal though. It was obviously never broadcasted, but the lenient sentence was likely because of some of his connections—doctors, people in government, that sort of thing."

"Okay, but if he's in jail—" Rachel started.

"Well, that's just the thing," Duvall said. She'd found what she was looking for and slowly turned the laptop to face Rachel. "His sentence was up three months ago. He's out."

Rachel leaned forward and looked at the mugshot of a man called Reginald Flournoy. He was very scrawny, his face long and gaunt looking. In the mugshot, his black hair hung down in his face and his large, dark eyes looked somehow bright and almost happy.

"Jesus, no wonder he went by an alias," Rachel said. "Any chance this address is accurate?"

"Doubtful. But I know a guy within the local DEA. Let me give him a call. I can pretty much guarantee you they've been keeping tabs on him if he only got out three months ago."

Duvall was already reaching for her phone and placing the call. Jack turned to Rachel, eyeing her with the sort of care that she was really starting to resent.

"Everything good in there?" he asked, nodding to the wall and the interrogation room on the other side.

"Yeah. I've got him sending a chain out for another party tonight. Just a back-up plan. I hope it won't come down to it, but you might want to get in the party mindset."

"Repetitive, electronic music out in the desert doesn't sound like much of a party," Jack said.

"Good thing we won't be going for the company."

Jack stepped closer to her and lowered his voice as Duvall started speaking on her phone. "Rach, you can get pissy with me if you want, but I have to ask. Are *you* okay from whatever happened in the car?"

She didn't even allow herself to get angry. Instead, she answered as honestly as she could without getting him worried. "The headache is still lurking but that's about it."

"Do you need to sit the rest of this out? Me and Duvall can—"

"No, Jack. I'm good."

"Will you tell me when you aren't?"

The anger almost leapt out, but she strangled it down when she reminded herself that he was only worried about her. And right now, it was more than just *her*. There was the case and the potential women to be saved.

"Yes, Jack. I promise, I'll tell you."

He opened his mouth to say something, but they both noticed that Duvall was already wrapping up her call. And there was a hint of excitement in her voice. She said goodbye to her DEA friend and ended the call, looking to them expectantly.

"We've got an address and confirmation that Lester is currently home right now. DEA is at the ready to roll out if we need an assist."

"Is he close by?"

"A small neighborhood just outside of the city—about a half an hour drive from here."

There was no discussion at all, no questions or planning. The three of them hurried out of the room and back through the station. The handful of officers on duty within the building watched them go as, once again, Rachel stepped back out into the desert heat with this case dangling yet another promising thread in front of her slowly failing eyes.

CHAPTER TWENTY THREE

Rachel had been expecting Lester to be located in a dwelling similar to the one they'd found Brett Alvarez living in. This was backed up by several years as a federal agent, where the majority of notorious drug dealers still elected to live in sprawls of urban decay and rundown apartments. So she found herself surprised when Duvall drove them into a suburban nook just fifteen miles outside of Albuquerque. It was the sort of subdivision that had its own pool, a basketball court, pickle ball courts, and a large clubhouse located in the center of it all.

"Looks like Lester invested some of his ill-begotten gains while in prison," Jack commented from the back seat.

"I'll say," Duvall replied. "It's a massive upgrade from the address that was listed on his pre-prison record."

"And your DEA buddy says there haven't been any instances of trouble?" Rachel asked as Duvall coasted by a chain of incredibly nice houses. Some of the houses had their own pools and massive garages.

"None so far. They have units that stay parked outside of his house every now and then. They don't keep a regular schedule so Lester can't easily predict when they are and aren't there."

"Will this be the first visit he's gotten from law enforcement?" Jack asked.

"No. They said there have been two teams that have stopped by on occasion just to do surprise checks. Then again, those were DEA agents. The presence of FBI agents might strike a different nerve, you know?"

That thought was left to weigh on their minds as Duvall parked their car along the sidewalk on the opposite side of the street from Lester's address. The house was gorgeous from the outside, the lower half made to look almost like shards of river rock and the rest a faded white brick. A huge cathedral window sat over the front door, which was accentuated with a minimalist porch.

Rachel couldn't shake the feeling of oddness that gripped her as they walked to the porch. She was quite sure she'd never knocked on the door to such an elaborate house in order to locate a drug dealer. She knocked and then took a step back, Jack angling in to take the lead.

Duvall waited a few steps behind, off to the side of the door so that she might not be immediately seen.

A loud, male voice from the other side of the door responded almost right away. "Yeah, hold on a second!"

They did just that, waiting with tense anticipation. After several seconds, they heard the sounds of an electric lock being disengaged. The door then opened, revealing pretty much the same image Rachel had seen in the police records. It almost looked as if Lester hadn't aged a day.

Lester eyed the three of them, catching Duvall at the last moment. He opened his mouth and asked what was a predictable question, but as the words left his mouth, Rachel also saw that by the time the last word was spoken, he already knew the answer.

"Yeah, who are you guys?"

"Are you Lester?" Jack asked. "Also known a Reginald Flournoy?"

Lester looked disgusted at the sound of his birth name and had already started to slowly shut the door.

"Who? Reginald what?"

"Fine," Jack said. "Lester. Are you Le—"

It happened so fast that the three of them stood momentarily dumbstruck. Lester closed the door in their face, slamming it hard before Jack could even finish the statement. When the confusion broke, Jack sneered at the door, took a step back, and threw his shoulder into it. His entire body shuddered as he rebounded.

"Not happening," he hissed. "That's *solid.*"

"Take the left," Duvall said, nodding to Rachel. And, in saying that, Duvall sprinted to the right and then around the side of the house.

Rachel pivoted and raced to the left. She heard Jack hissing her name behind her, probably wanting to ask her if she was sure she should be running. But by that time, the adrenaline was running. In sensing there was some form of law enforcement at his door, Lester had chosen to close them out. It meant not only guilt, but guilt over something he would likely be in a lot of trouble for.

She came to the corner of the house and turned left. There, she found a sizable strip of yard that was separated from the neighboring yard by a row of unruly hedges. As she started across this strip of grass, she heard a slight banging sound from up ahead and around the back of the house. A door closing, but not with any great deal of force. Apparently, Lester was trying to make a run for it—which seemed like a foolish prospect in a neighborhood where the property lines were so close together.

But also a neighborhood Lester knew far better than they did. This thought kicked Rachel into another gear, as the backside of the house drew closer. And as she neared the back, she saw Lester racing to the backside of his property. It looked out over onto the back yard of another house, the two properties separated by a beautiful, black iron fence. As Rachel came to the back yard, Lester was approaching it. It was too high up to jump over, but it wouldn't take much scaling.

She also saw that Duvall had a bit of a lead on her. She was also barreling for the fence, her hand hovering over her sidearm, not sure if she should draw it yet. "FBI!" she yelled! "Stop right there!"

But Lester clearly had no intention of stopping. He had reached the fence, leaping up on it and nearly making it over. But he had to grab the top at the last minute and haul himself over. As he did, Duvall caught up to him and grabbed him by the waist. Lester wasted no time in fighting her off, throwing an elbow back behind him. He nailed Duvall in the top of the head, causing her to buckle just enough to release him.

As Duvall stumbled back, Lester made his way over the top of the fence. At the same time, Rachel leaped up onto it, her fingers nearly grazing the back of Lester's shirt. She hauled herself up, her feet scaling the iron rails of the fence, and placed her foot along the top. Throwing caution to the wind and giving into her admittedly reckless streak, she leaped straight out, pushing off of the top in what was essentially a suicide dive.

She was weightless for about two seconds as she sailed over into the neighboring yard. But even before she started coming down, she knew her aim had been true. Lester looked back just in time to see her rocketing towards him. The two of them collided in a painful heap, Rachel hitting with such impact that she bounced right off of his back as Lester slammed into the ground. The jolt sent a black veil over her vision and for a moment, Rachel was sure the headache was going to come back. She scrambled to her feet, her head swimming. The veil swept away as she blinked her eyes, but she also noted that her vision in her right eye looked like nothing more than a smear of fuzzy color now.

No, she thought. *No...not now, please...just a while longer, pl—*

She didn't see Lester's right hand coming at her head until it had already connected. It took her right in the chin. She heard her teeth clink together and then she was falling. And even as she fell, she reached out, trying to stop him from running away.

"Hey!"

She heard Jack's voice, yelling in rage as he went racing by. The punch to the head and the faulty vision didn't allow her to see him, but she felt the stirring of wind as he passed by. She then heard another collision and Jack's angry voice.

"You make another move and I swear I'll purposefully break your wrist when I put these cuffs on you."

Rachel started to stagger back to her feet, her vision still not improving. She took a step forward but then Duvall was there, at her side. She put an arm under Rachel's arm, which Rachel allowed for a moment.

"You okay, Agent Gift?"

"Yeah, I'm fine," she said. But she was already opening and closing her jaw to make sure she hadn't broken it or cracked it. She then ran her tongue along the backsides of her teeth, making sure none had been loosened. She counted herself lucky; not only had Lester punched her while moving away from her, but he looked to weigh just above the heft of a scarecrow.

Slowly, everything came back into focus. She saw Jack yanking Lester to his feet, the man's hands cuffed behind him. There was a grass stain on the side of his head. Jack shoved Lester to the black, iron gate with a shove of fury. He then turned his eyes to Rachel and the softened a bit.

"You okay?" he asked.

"Yeah, I think so. Just a little rattled. Fortunately, he can't hit for shit."

"All the same, I want you to sit down and—"

"Jack, I'm not—"

"Damn it, Rachel! I'm not arguing about this. You sit down and take a rest right now. I'm going to throw this scumbag into the back of the car and then Duvall and I are going to have a look in his house."

"The hell you are!" Lester screamed from the fence.

Jack started charging at him but then caught himself. He muttered a stream of curses under his breath. The entire scene quieted Lester. He talked as if he might be able to take down an army but flinched so easily that Rachel assumed he'd been the target of a lot of ass-kickings over the course of his life.

"Okay, fine," Rachel said. "Just…I'll stay here, standing against the fence."

"And you're okay?" he asked, his tone lighter now. "For real?"

She nodded but found it hard to look at him—not only because he'd never snapped at her like that, but also because focusing on anything

120

for more than just a second or two was a reminder that the vision in her right eye was quickly deteriorating.

CHAPTER TWENTY FOUR

By the time Rachel, Jack, and Duvall returned to the precinct and hour and a half later, the vision in Rachel's right eye was completely gone. It wasn't as if she were operating blind; the vision in her left eyes was as impeccable as usual, and she was able to walk and function as she always did. If anything, what was really bothering her the most was the aching along the curve of her chin where Lester had hit her. It had bruised slightly and was aching just enough to be a constant nuisance.

They opted to take Lester back to the Foxham police department, despite the fact that it was fifteen miles further away than the closest Albuquerque station. They'd been using it as their temporary base of operations, and it just seemed more convenient and comfortable. By the time they got back, Brett Alvarez had been released. A woman at the front desk was quick to wave Rachel down when they arrived, giving her a printed sheet of paper where Alverez had indicated the coordinates of tonight's hastily planned rave in the desert.

Rachel looked it over while Jack and Duvall escorted Lester to the interrogation room Alvarez had been occupying up until about twenty minutes ago. He was fighting against them and screaming, drawing enough attention that two officers rushed over to give them an assist. Studying the print-out she'd been handed, Rachel saw that someone had printed out the map and everything. It showed the coordinates and how to get there. In the bottom left corner, someone had even scrawled *1 a.m.*

"When was Mr. Alvarez released?" she asked.

"Oh, not quite half an hour ago, I'd say," the woman behind the desk said.

"Did he give anyone any problems?"

"None that I saw."

Rachel folded the sheet of paper and stuffed it into her pocket. "Thank you."

She slowly made her way to the interrogation room. Jack and Duvall had already gone in, the door left partially open. For a fleeting and scary moment, Rachel considered calling Jack out into the hallway. She needed to tell him about her vision, about that black veil that had come down over her eyes for a terrifying moment after she'd taken down Lester. She figured she at least owed it to him. At this point, she was basically a liability.

She paused at the door and opened her mouth to say something. She thought of Paige, back home. What if the rest of her vision went and she was never able to see her daughter again? What if she didn't take care of herself and she died, leaving Paige and maybe even Grandma Tate to constantly worry about the threatening letters and actions Alex Lynch was somehow sending out from his prison cell?

Duvall's raised voice broke Rachel out of her thoughts. "It's just questions for right now but if you keep this up, it's going to make us a hell of a lot more suspicious!"

"You already went through my house, which I did *not* give you permission to do!"

"Ah, but we barely went through your house," Jack rebuffed. "Based on your attitude during the ride here, we now have a few cops searching your place."

"Both of you can go to hell!" Lester said.

It was here that Rachel finally stepped into the room. Talking to Jack about her vision was out of the question now. They had a case to work on. And while it was very clear that Duvall was fully capable of subbing in for her, Rachel could not quit. She understood that it was stubborn and maybe even selfish. But she felt that the case was going to close soon—whether it came as a direct result of whatever they got out of Lester or tonight at the rave—and she could not bow out now. Though, when the time did come, she knew she had a very big decision to make.

When Rachel stepped in, Lester focused his gaze on her. "And you…I should get you for assault."

"Good luck with that. You were actively running from federal agents after we did nothing more than knock on your door. We had just cause."

"Yeah, we'll see what my lawyer says about that."

"Yes, please, let's see what he says," Rachel said. She looked to Duvall and Jack, making sure she wasn't trying *too* hard to make it seem like she was perfectly fine. Perfectly normal. "You hit me, an FBI agent. You hit me because we came knocking on your door. Your lawyer is sure to *love* that."

"Look, I'm not stupid. I know why you were there, at my house. I know what you wanted. And even when you looked through the place, you didn't find anything now did you?"

"We did not," Duvall said. "But that doesn't make sense because…well, you *ran.* Let's get back to that. Why would you run from us, unprovoked, if you weren't hiding something?"

Lester didn't answer. Rachel looked to Duvall and shrugged. "Want to get his lawyer on the line?"

"Sure," Duvall said, heading for the door.

"Or," Jack said, "we can talk to him right now and leave the lawyer out of it. The lawyer, the punching the face of a federal agent, all of it. What do you say to that, Agent Gift?"

The ease in which the three of them slid into this concocted set-up was impressive. Not knowing Duvall all that well, Rachel just hoped she'd be able to keep a straight face.

"He punched me," she said. "No. Call his lawyer."

"Gift…," Jack said. "Come on. The lawyer comes in, it takes too long, will hold us up. You know how it goes. Don't let it waste more of your time. It's just a few questions anyway, right?"

Rachel looked back to Lester and saw that he was buying it. There was some relief in his eyes, but his hands were still clenching and unclenching on the table as he tried to suppress his anger.

"Five minutes," she said. She then made a huge, dramatic display of walking to the back of the room, her arms folded over her chest. It worked out well, as it also gave her a moment to collect herself. She was worried about her vision and health, but also sensed that this could potentially turn out to be an important interrogation.

With Rachel at the back of the room, it was Jack that stepped forward and took the lead.

"I'm going to start with the most basic question," Jack said. "Why *did* you run when the FBI came knocking on your door?"

"I don't even know, man. Shit, you know my history, right? It's bad enough the DEA comes by whenever they want, just to look around my place. But I knew you guys were something different. You just…well, you *look* like FBI agents. And I freaked out. I got scared and ran."

"Here's the thing," Jack said. "I don't believe that. But we'll leave it to the cops that are currently at your house to turn up anything we may have missed in our rush. Besides that, there are bigger questions we have for you. We're currently working on a case that deals with hallucinogenic drugs and—"

"And you figured I was responsible because of my past? Unless you missed the news, I've been in prison for the last little stretch of time."

"Yes, I know. But the thing is, we have someone that saw you on the scene of a suspected kidnapping."

"Kidnapping? I thought this was about drugs."

Duvall sighed and nodded. "It is. Three women have been murdered recently, and they had all traces of psychedelic drugs in their system. And as of right now you are the only known drug dealer to have been spotted on the scene."

"Spotted by who?" he said, his anger coming out more and more.

"We obviously can't tell you that," Jack said. "But again, if you truly have nothing to hide, you call tell us about any parties you've been to, right?"

"Yeah, I can. Because I haven't done any dealing since I left prison."

"You're sure about that?"

"Yeah, look…I've done some messed up stuff over the years, but if you guys are trying to find a killer, I'm just not your guy."

Jack was on the cusp of saying something else when there was a knock on the door. One of the assisting officers opened the door and poked his head in. He looked to Duvall and beckoned her outside. She left quickly, closing the door behind her.

"Mister…*Lester*," Jack said. "Be honest with us, okay? We know you've been to some parties recently. Some parties out in the desert. Will you agree to that?"

"Yeah, I can agree to that. But like I said, I'm not deal—"

"And for these parties, are you contacted individually, or are you part of a text chain of people that are invited to these parties?"

Lester showed a bit of caution here, taking a moment to think about his reply before giving it. "There's a text thread that goes out from some guy that organizes them. But I don't even know that many of the people at those things even do psychedelics. Maybe a few here and there but not like they used to."

"Is that where you had the most success when you were a prominent dealer?" Jack asked.

"Yeah."

"So what you're saying is that even if you *did* decide to pick up your old habits, you're saying these parties wouldn't be worth the trouble?"

"Not for me, no. Maybe for some small-time dealers, just getting started."

Rachel continued to listen. She was impressed with how Jack was leading to their main point. Jack was expertly laying out a trap and it didn't seem that Lester had any idea at all.

"What about murderers?" Jack asked. "Everyone we've talked to about these little parties...they're sort of biased. They all seem to think it's just unbelievable to think someone may be using these parties to kidnap and kill people."

Rachel saw him stiffen, saw Lester's eyes get shifty. The question had made him very nervous now that they were back on the topic of murders. Still, he tried to hold in ground. "I don't think so, man. No, I mean, I think it's mostly for what some people call a new hippie movement. Peace, love, music. That sort of thing."

Rachel stepped slowly away from the wall and locked eyes with him. "In your line of work, have you met any killers?"

"If I did, I wasn't aware of it."

"And have you ever heard of men using hallucinogenic and psychedelics as a sort of a tranquilizer?"

"Yeah," he said, clearly uncomfortable now. "I know a lot of guys that stopped selling certain types of ecstasy because they were being used as a sort of date rape drug."

Rachel was prepared to keep going, but the door opened again. It was Duvall, coming back into the room. She had a single sheet of paper in her hand and though Rachel could not quite put her finger on it, something about Duvall's entire expression had changed.

"I'd like to ask Lester a question, if that's okay," Duvall said.

"Of course," Jack said, stepping aside and letting her stand directly in front of the table.

Duvall looked like she was straddling a line between nervousness and excitement. It made Rachel think that whatever had been said to her outside might be a case-breaker.

"Lester, do you know a woman named Valerie Mitcham?"

At the start of the question, especially at the word *woman*, Lester grew visibly tense. His jaw clenched and he sat so rigidly in his chair that Rachel figured everything within him must have tightened up. Something had definitely been triggered.

But then there was a small moment of relief. Carefully, he shook his head. "No. Don't know a woman by that name."

"Then why was your number listed in her phone contacts?"

With that bomb dropped, Duvall turned to face Rachel and Jack. "When we called the arrest in, I had the guys look into the phone records of our three victims to see if Lester was listed on any of them. We got a hit with Valerie Mitcham."

"And the others?" Jack asked.

"No. Nothing on them."

"Wait, what the hell are you even talking about?" Lester said. "I just told you I don't know anyone by that name."

"Okay, well let me give you another one, then," Duvall said. "How about Simone Switzer? That one ring a bell?"

Lester looked like someone had reached out and punched him right in the chest. He gave them a perplexed look and then did his best to redirect. "Make up your minds! Do you want to know about drugs or this Valerie lady, or this Switzer lady? Choose one!"

"I think I'd like to know about the Switzer lady," Rachel said.

"Simone Switzer," Duvall said. "When Lester here was taken into custody just before heading to prison, a small ledger-style book was found in his apartment. There were six names circled and highlighted—people that owed him money for drugs. He admitted this much on the stand. Turns out, one of the names was Valerie Mitcham. We know what happened to her. The other was a woman named Simone Switzer."

"So are you saying there's a fourth victim out there somewhere?" Jack asked.

"Oh, no. Simone Switzer was found dead almost a month ago. In her home. Stabbed repeatedly in the heart and found on her kitchen floor. And a third woman in that same book—named Padma Behera—has been missing for about two weeks now."

"Padma left for India right after I got out of prison!"

They all turned to him following this outburst. He gritted his teeth and cursed, knowing full well he'd said too much. He glanced up to them with hatred and sincere worry in his eyes. After taking a deep breath, he said: "I'd like to speak with my lawyer now."

CHAPTER TWENTY FIVE

The three agents sat in the breakroom of the Foxham police department as evening drifted in outside, dropping the heat down roughly ten degrees. Rachel and Jack drank coffees while Duvall sipped on a Coke. Duvall had gone into the database and found photocopies of the book where the six names had been circled and highlighted. Valerie Mitcham had apparently been doing drugs much longer than anyone had expected. Her name was in the book and now she was dead, her heart torn right out of her body.

The name Simone Switzer was also there, circled and highlighted. Rachel was currently looking through the crime scene reports and looking for anything that might resemble the bodies they'd found out in the desert. Other than the heart being targeted, there seemed to be nothing. There was certainly nothing about the murder that screamed "Aztec ritual."

And then there was Padma Behera. From what they could tell based on phone records and a quick call to her landlord, she had indeed left the country a little less than three months ago. And yes, it did seem to coincide with Lester's release from prison. It made Rachel wonder what, exactly, was so scary about the scrawny little creep that would make a woman leave the country. Maybe she'd known what he was capable of. Maybe if Padma could see the crime scene photos from Simone Switzer's house, she may not be all that surprised.

As she looked through the case files, she saw that there had been some written speculation that Switzer's death may be linked to Lester's recent prison release. She wondered why nothing had been followed up on. Or maybe that was why the DEA had been doing random checks—that, among other things.

While she read, she also noticed Agent Duvall sneaking peeks over at Jack every now and then. Jack was zoned out, coffee in one hand and a pen in the other. He was doodling on a small legal pad, something he often did when trying to declutter his brain and find a clear path to pursue.

"So what I'm wondering," Duvall said suddenly, "is if we can dig into Lester's current client list to see who the other victims might be. Anyone who owes him money would be a clear target, right?"

"I was thinking the same thing," Jack said. He looked up from his doodles and his eyes met with Duvall's for a moment. He didn't blush, but he may as well have. Rachel was pretty sure she'd never seen such a bashful smile on Jack's face before.

"But what concerns me," Jack went on, "is that this murder case with Simone Switzer seemed to be lackluster at best in terms of how it was handled. I know Lester supposedly had high-ranking clients and friends, but would it be enough to not even really press on him when this woman was found dead not too long after he escaped from prison?"

"It's a good question, and worth looking into," Duvall said. "If this creep goes to trial for all of this, I think it needs to be at least reconsidered."

"Is there a lot of police corruption around here?" Jack asked.

"No more than anywhere else in the country."

They shared another look and this time it was Duvall that offered the bashful smile. Before Rachel was fully aware of what she was doing, she got to her feet. She gave a quick *"Excuse me,"* and left the breakroom with her coffee in hand. When she was standing in the hall, she had no idea where she was going. Not to the interrogation rooms, that was for sure. In the end, she headed for the front doors and walked outside, pulling her phone from her pocket. Checking the time, she thought Grandma Tate should be back home with Paige right about now. When she scrolled to find the contact, she was again reminded of the lack of vision in her right eye. She fought down a wave of self-pity and she FaceTimed Grandma Tate, taking a seat on a small bench in front of the station.

The call took a while to connect and when it was answered, it was Paige's face that greeted her. Her heart churned at the sight of Paige's bright, shining face. She was sweating a bit and had the remnants of a recent snack around the rim of her mouth.

"Hey, Mommy!"

"Hey, sweetie. How are you?"

"I'm good. Me and Grandma Tate are outside, playing croquet."

"Croquet? We have croquet?"

"Yeah, I guess."

Then Grandma Tate's voice came from somewhere in the background. "Yeah, it was in that deathtrap of a garage, hiding behind the equally neglected cornhole boards."

Rachel cringed internally at the mention of the cornhole boards. They were a. purchase Peter had made, insisting it was something they could do as a family on nice summer days in the back yard. In the end, they'd used them three times and then they'd sat in the garage, collecting dust. A lot of Peter's last-minute, spontaneous purchases had ended up that way.

"Did you have a good day at school?"

"Yeah! I got a perfect score on our spelling test and there were *thirty* words!"

"Way to go!" She found herself struggling not to cry. She didn't even know Paige had a spelling test coming up. God, when was the last time she'd sat down with her daughter and helped with her homework?

This has got to stop, she thought. *If you make it through this case, this has got to be it. You have very little time left and you need to stop being selfish—you need to spend the rest of the time you have left with your daughter.*

"Do you know when you'll be home?"

"It shouldn't be much longer. It's looking like things might be wrapping up soon. There's a very good chance I could be back home as early as tomorrow night, but you know how it goes. I can't—"

"I know, I know. You can't make any promises."

"That's right. Hey, can I talk to Grandma Tate really quick?"

"Sure. Bye. I love you!"

"I love you, too." But, as usual, the phone was already moving before Paige had a chance to hear those four words. After a few seconds, Grandma Tate was looking into the camera. She was also sweating, but she looked happy.

"I overhear that your case looks to be closing?"

"That's the hope. If something changes and I'm going to be more than another day or so, I'll let you know." She hesitated here, noticing that slowly, some of the vision in her right eye was starting to come back. It was very hazy, like looking at the world through a plastic bottle, but it was better than seeing nothing at all.

"You look beat," Grandma Tate said. "Is it…well, is it a *bad* case?"

"Yeah, it's pretty grim. How about you? Are you feeling okay?"

"Oh, I am. Paige is keeping me on my toes. And I won't even lie about it; I came back to your house from taking her to school and slept another three hours. It was bliss."

"And what about the—"

"I'm fine, Rachel. It's one of those days where the only reason I know I have it is because I was diagnosed. I feel perfectly fine. How about you?" Her glare was filled with accusation, as if she somehow *knew* about the driving incident and the difficulty with her right eye.

"I'm good. I think I feel a little more tired than usual, but it's fine."

130

"And you're still planning on telling...certain people...when you get back home?"

"Yes," she said, finding that she once again had to fight back tears. "It might take me a few days to recover from what's going on here, but yes. I am." She feared that she was going to break down at any moment, so she stood up and acted as if she had somewhere to be. "I should get going. Thanks again for stepping in."

"Oh, don't mention it. I'm having the time of my life over here!"

Rachel said her goodbyes and ended the call. She took a moment, taking in a deep breath of the surprisingly cool evening air. She closed her eyes, counted to three, and opened them. The vision was still blurry in her right eye but it seemed to be coming back slowly.

Before she had a chance to turn back around to the doors, they opened up as someone came out. It was Jack, habitually still carrying the pen he had been doodling with. He crossed his arms in a show of mock defiance and stared her down.

"What's going on, Rachel?"

"Nothing. I'm just beat. And if you want the truth, yes. I'm still a little rattled over the incident in the car." She found that she was fine in admitting that so long as it kept him satisfied and not pressing any harder. She no longer wanted to tell him about what was going on with her eye. She wasn't sure why but the obvious growing connection between him and Duvall had her looking at the case differently. With the two of them starting to gel, the last thing she wanted to be was the weak link that slowed things down. She figured that one way or the other, she would manage to finish this case out—even if she did have to take something of a backseat to Duvall for the last stage.

Besides, it was her hope that it was all but over. Once Lester's lawyer got in, they'd know more. It would also help if there was some sort of development with forensics or phone records that would really slam the last nail in Lester's coffin. But for all the hand wringing and coffee-fueled planning the three of them had done in the breakroom, there didn't seem to be a single, easy connection.

"Are you sure that's all?" he asked, not willing to back down as easily as usual.

She hated to do it, but she decided the only way to get him off the scent of her uneasiness would be to toss some awkward home situations at him. She knew it was borderline manipulative but, in that moment, she just needed him to back off. Aware that she had snapped at him far too often over the last few weeks, that was the last thing she wanted to do. But if he kept pushing, she knew it was coming.

"I think I already told you, but I left Paige with my grandmother. I'm just a little worried about them. But I just spoke with both of them, and things seem to be going well."

"Well, you know, we're just waiting for his stupid lawyer to show up. If you want, just chill out for the rest of the time. I think Duvall and I can handle it from here."

She hated how much it hurt to hear him say that. But she took it on her already sore chin and reached for the door.

"She does seem really smart," Rachel commented.

"It also helps that she knows the area well. It weird, though, that she can't seem to recall any recent drug busts that involved peyote."

They walked back inside and as Rachel passed through the doorway, she paused. "Yeah," she said, thinking. "Peyote…that really doesn't fit, does it?"

"I mean, it does in that it's a hallucinogen in some respects."

"No, I mean in the eyes of a dealer. Think about it, Jack. How many drug busts have you personally been a part of?"

He chuckled as his eyes got wide. "At least twenty."

"And in each of those cases, how many of the dealers offered variety? Sure, it happens here and there. Maybe your pot dealer is also your coke dealer, but if that *is* the case, he's going to have a much higher supply of one rather than the other, right?"

"Yeah…?"

"But in the grand scheme of things, successful dealers tend to stick with one drug—with what they know. Would you agree to that?"

"Yeah, for sure. That's a safe assumption."

Slowly, it dawned on him. But even before he said anything, there was doubt on his face. "I know where you're going with it, but all three of the drugs we've found in the victims were all psychedelics. Maybe *that's* his specialty. I doubt he'd close himself off to juts *one* kind."

"Maybe. But the peyote is what's throwing me off. Duvall said Lester was known for even assisting some researchers with small doses of psychedelics. I know some places are experimenting with MDMA and even DMT. Peyote, though…that's mescaline, right? I mean, at its core."

"I think so. Rachel, what are you—"

"Let's go have a chat with Lester really quick."

"His lawyer isn't here yet."

"Do I care?" she asked, slightly annoyed. She hurried back to the interrogation rooms. When she walked back into Lester's room, she saw that he'd been granted a cup of coffee. As she took her place in the chair in front of the table, Jack also entered the room.

"Nice to see you again," Lester said, "but you don't get another word out of me until my lawyer gets here."

"I don't have time for that," Rachel spat. "Besides, these aren't going to be incriminating questions. I just have some questions about drugs."

"I don't care. I'm not—"

"What can you tell me about peyote?"

This seemed to confuse Lester for a moment. He looked as her as if she had just asked the strangest question he'd ever heard. "What do you think I am, some sort of Wikipedia for drugs?"

"Maybe, for all I know. Peyote. Have you ever dealt it?"

"I did when I was getting started, like almost ten years ago. But there's not much street demand for it anymore. Anyone that really wants it usually has ins with some of the Native American tribes a little further west so it's pretty common in most circles out this way. Also, it's not the cleanest high unless you're getting it right from the source."

"The source being what?" Jack asked, now also curious.

"Some special kind of cactus."

"And you haven't dealt it since you had your prison sentence?"

"Not since *long* before my prison sentence."

Even though there was the distinct possibility that Lester had indeed killed Simone Switzer and he deserved to be sitting where he currently sat, Rachel understood that he was not *their* killer. A man like Lester, if he was indeed back to dealing even under the watchful eye of the DEA, took pride in his work. Would he really muddy the waters of his trade and reputation by dealing a drug he considered to be subpar? Of course, he could just be lying. In the long run, she figured it didn't really matter. If things ended up clean, he'd be held for the murder he *had* committed, so he was going to be here for a while.

Rachel didn't bother with a closing question or further arguments. She simply walked away, leaving the interrogation room yet again. Duvall was standing in the hallway, directly between the interrogation room and the break room.

"Is everything okay?" she asked.

"Yeah, we're fine," Jack said. "Agent Gift just sort of has a knack for this."

"A knack for what, exactly?"

"Moments of clarity that come in at just the right moment."

"Clarity? Do you...do you think Lester isn't our guy?"

Rachel stamped down her irritation, realizing that she was only annoyed with Duvall because she was getting Jack's attention. It was childish and selfish, and she wished she could just shut it down.

"I don't." She reached into her pocket and took out the sheet she'd been handed by the woman at the front desk, the paper with the location of Brett Alvarez's rave. "Fortunately, I have a back-up plan, though."

"At the risk of sounding bossy, can I be filled in?" Duvall asked.

"Ah," Jack said with a smile. "Finally, someone that knows how I feel." Then, looking to Rachel with the same level of trust he usually displayed towards her, he said: "What have you got?"

CHAPTER TWENTY SIX

The three agents sat at a corner booth at Rose's Grill, waiting on their dinner orders to arrive. It was just past 8:00, and it hadn't taken long for Rachel to fill them in on her theory. She was relieved to find that they were both on board. She also took note that Jack and Duvall seemed to almost make a point to sit beside one another. She spied on them with her still-suffering vision and wondered if Jack might be making quite a few calls and video chats back out this way when they returned home.

"Look, Rachel," Jack said. "I won't say this is a stretch, but you understand that he could simply be lying to us, right? He's a potential murderer and has a history of drug dealing."

"Yes, I do understand that. But I think we also let the presence of drugs blind us." She cringed internally at her choice of words, as her right eye was still not clear. "We had that one solid link and ran with it. But this case was never about drugs. It's about women being killed, dragged into the desert, and having their hearts removed."

She could tell that Jack was already leaning in her direction of thought; he'd worked enough cases to know how she worked—to know that these last-minute hunches tended to be accurate more times than not. She watched as Agent Duvall considered the theory and thought she had her, too.

"It would explain why there was no evidence of murder at his house," she said. "Some of the cops are still over there, you know. Now, I was never expecting to roll up in the killer's home and find three Mason jars with hearts stuffed into them, but I also wasn't quite ready to give up on Lester being our guy, either."

"The way I see it," Rachel said, "he and his lawyer can sit there and talk to the cops all night. His name being in Valerie's phone and the fact that he punched me gives us enough weight to hold him for another day or so. In the meantime, there's no harm in checking this." She tapped at the sheet of paper that sat on the table between them.

"And you think he'll come through for us?" Jack asked.

"I think he'd be an idiot not to. If he lied to me about this, it just gives us one more reason to haul him back in tomorrow."

The waitress brought their dinners over and it wasn't until Rachel saw the bacon cheeseburger in front of her that she realized just how hungry she was. She started eating before Jack and Duvall had gotten their food. As soon as they all settled in and started eating, Duvall picked up a French fry and used it to point at the sheet of paper.

"Well, I'm definitely in," she said. "More than that, I think I should be the one to attend the party."

"No, I can take that on," Rachel argued.

"It should be me. You and Rivers here have been flashing your badges all over town. There's too big of a chance that someone will blow your cover. Also, you were all over Alvarez today. There's no way he's going to see you there and not be acting strange. A few wayward looks and people might get paranoid—assuming they'd see the behavior *before* the drugs kick in." She popped the fry in her mouth, looked to both of them, and shrugged innocently. "Also, no offense to either of you, but I'm the youngest of the three of us."

"Not by much," Jack argued, smirking at her.

"I'll dress appropriately, make sure I look the part," Duvall said. "Back in my younger days, I did enjoy the occasional rave. I don't even mind the music all that much."

"Have you ever done undercover before?" Rachel asked.

"Twice. Once for a minor drug bust and a second time when a small team that I was on worked to bust up a prostitution ring."

Rachel looked to Jack and, though she was pretty sure she knew what his answer would be, she said: "What do you think?"

"I think I'm hurt that she thinks she looks younger than I am. But I also think she's right. If Alvarez is there and spots you even if he *is* expecting you, I think he may end up behaving unpredictably."

"Okay, then," Rachel said. "If you're sure you're up for it, let's do that." She was surprised to find that she was nervous for Duvall. It was more than not being able to be the one in control of the situation. Though Rachel wasn't sure how she felt about the blossoming interest between Duvall and Jack, Duvall had been a massive help on this case. Rachel wanted only the best for her, and that included safety.

Jack looked to the sheet, staring at the grainy map. He then opened up the maps app on his phone and found the exact same spot. He zoomed in, using his finger to navigate to the spot. There were two roads that bordered the site of the night's party, one coming in from a secondary road that led into Albuquerque. The other was one of several roads that seemed to wander through the desert with no clear destination in mind. It connected to other roads just like the maze of small roads connected with the two-lane that made its way through Foxham.

"Are you familiar with both of these roads?" Jack asked.

"Somewhat. This one," she said, pointing to the long and winding one that meandered aimlessly through the desert, "is something of a nightmare for local law enforcement in terms of catching speeders."

"So where would be the best place for Jack and I to wait until you need an assist?"

"I think that would be right here," she said, pointing to an area just off the road. "If memory serves, there should be this old pull-over spot that looks out onto a rock formation locals call The Three Brothers. From what I can tell, this party spot is close enough to there."

"All the same, I think we should ride out and get a lay of the land," Rachel said. "The party doesn't start until after midnight. We've still got four and a half hours."

They fell into silence for a moment, the only noise the clinking of silverware on plates. After a while, Duvall broke it. She looked back and forth between them and asked, "You guys sure this is okay? I really don't want to be a third wheel. It's clear you guys have worked together for a while."

"Not at all," Rachel said. What she thought, but did not say, was: *No, I think it's me that's the third wheel.* "You've been a godsend for this entire case."

The smile on Duvall's face after this comment seemed genuine and once again, Rachel was aware of Jack's eyes on her. She was happy for him but, at the same time, was starting to feel protective of him. It wasn't in any romantic way, but almost the same way a sister would be protective of a brother falling for a strange woman.

She ignored it for the moment, choosing to give Agent Duvall the benefit of the doubt. Instead, she chose to look out of the diner window, out into the darkening desert night and wondered what their killer might be doing at that very moment.

***

The secondary road Duvall had pointed out on the map also provided several access roads. During their initial search of the place, they'd discovered that most of these roads were dead ends, while others were state maintained and basically used for the highway department. The secondary road took them into the most desolate stretch of desert

Rachel had seen yet, made all the more eerie given the darkness of night.

They'd first seen the silhouettes of The Three Brothers at 8:40 as they went through their initial search. With Duvall driving and Rachel sitting in the passenger seat, Duvall had pointed them out, pointing across to Rachel's window. Only two of them had appeared at first, standing out against the darkness. As they passed along a bit further, the third one appeared from behind the much larger middle one.

Another access road had presented itself half a mile later. It etched in toward the Three Brothers, coming to a stop a good distance away. By their best estimate, the end of the access road was a little over half a mile away from where Brett Alvarez planned to have tonight's party.

The trio looked out in that direction now, just three hours after having seen it for the first time. They'd elected to park on a road further out, assuming most of the party's attendees would parking at the end of the road that looked out onto The Three Brothers. They were driving Duvall's personal car, a newer model Honda Civic. With the ignition off and the three of them standing outside of the car, Jack chuckled.

"What's funny?" Rachel said.

"Duvall."

Agent Duvall turned to him with a look on her face that even Rachel saw as cute. "And what the hell is so funny?" Duvall asked.

"Well, it's not *funny.*" He looked her up and down, taking in her far-too baggy, dark jeans and her tank top. The top fit her well, showing off curves that had not been visible for the earlier portions of the case. "The outfit…well, it suits you."

"I wasn't sure how to dress for this. I didn't think the psychedelic crowd would be impressed with my Van Halen or Nirvana t-shirts."

"Van Halen?" Jack said. "I mean, would *anyone* be impressed with that?"

Before Duvall could respond, a light beeping sound reached their ears. Duvall pulled her phone out of her pocket and shut her alarm off. She'd set it to go off at 11:55, which would give her enough time to prep and then make the walk out to the site of the party. From where they were currently parked, it would take her about twenty minutes make the walk to the party site.

"Okay, here goes nothing," Duvall said. She reached into the car and took out the small clip-on microphone she'd taken from the Foxham PD. She reached up into her tank top and awkwardly worked to get it clipped to the side of her bra.

Jack opened the car door, sat in the passenger seat, and cut on the portable radio. The radio had been rushed to the Foxham PD at the very last minute, as there had not been a functioning one in Foxham.

"Testing," Duvall said, speaking at a normal volume.

Jack nodded from inside the car. "Got it loud and clear." He stepped back out, starting to look rather nervous. "Just make sure you keep testing as you make your way to the site. Remember, it's just a one-way, so if we lose connection, we're going to have to come in. We'll stay right at the rim of the party area, but..."

He shrugged here, clearly hoping it would not come to that.

"We'll call the station and alert them that you're leaving," Rachel said. "Both Foxham and Albuquerque. If the killer shows up here tonight and somehow manages to get away, he won't make it far."

"And one more time," Jack said. "What's the code word?"

"For the hundredth time," Duvall said, feigning annoyance, "it's *ink pen.*"

"Okay," Jack said, still looking worried. "Have fun working that into conversation when the time comes.

Duvall gave them a nervous smile, her eyes lingering on Jack a bit longer than Rachel. The gaze that locked between Duvall and Jack was so intense that Rachel made herself look away. She called up the Foxham police department and put them on alert. The officer she spoke with volunteered to put the word in to Albuquerque as well.

When she was done on the phone, she looked down the slight decline to the ground, watching Duvall's figure start to blend in with the darkness of the desert. "She'll be fine," Rachel said, speaking to Jack more than to herself.

"Yeah, I think so, too," Jack said. "You know, there's something about her personality that reminds me of you from a few years back."

She tried to remember what she'd been like five or six years ago. A little more carefree, sure. More willing to take unnecessary risks while, at the same time, a little more prone to ass-kissing those above her. And, of course, she'd bene unhindered by the knowledge that there was a tumor in her brain that was affecting her vision, causing headaches, and would ultimately take her life in about a year or so. Maybe sooner.

"Jack?"

"Yeah?" He was still looking out into the darkness where they could no longer see Duvall.

"I really am okay. For now. When we get back home, maybe I'll cool it off. To think that I could have seriously hurt or even killed you in that car today...it's unforgivable."

"Yeah, it is," he said. "Because I've already forgiven you. I'm just worried about you, Rachel. I'm used to only seeing you strong—strong and in control. I think it's just harder than I thought to accept the fact that you might have a weakness."

She looked out into the dark desert, much like staring out to the sea at night. Before she could think of anything to say, she heard something very far away, off in the distance. At first, she thought it might be summer thunder, the sort that is nothing more than grumbling from the sky. But after a few seconds, she realized that it was the soft echo and reverberation of music coming from somewhere in the desert.

The party had started.

Another noise came from behind them. It was Duvall's voice at low volume. "You guys hear that? Music, from up ahead. And as I get closer, there's...there are a few people headed that way. I see a group of three angling in from the right...another couple behind them."

Jack began to pace by the side of the car. "I don't like this," he said. "There are far too many uncertainties."

"There are," Rachel agreed. "But we'll hear them."

"I don't like that the communication is just one way."

"We've been over this," Rachel said. "And Duvall agreed. Two-way would be too risky. Someone could hear or see, or—"

"I know," he said.

"You like her?"

"Yeah, I think I do," he said, not bothering to even pretend otherwise. "But I'd be just as nervous about this set-up if it was someone I didn't like."

"I know." This was true, though it was also nice to see him so attached to someone. Jack had always been the sort that cared for others, but Rachel wasn't sure if she'd ever seen him romantically interested in anyone.

Together, they stared out into the night. The music droned on in the distance and after a while, Rachel thought she could make out the murky flickering of a fire. She supposed if she had full vision in both her eyes, she'd know for sure.

"See the fire out there?" she said. "Is that what it is?"

"Yeah, a bonfire, I suppose. For the party."

They said nothing else for a while, but the silence was broken on occasion by Duvall's voice reporting in. In whispers, she told them where she was, how many other people she was passing and then finally, the most important message of all.

"Okay, guys. I'm here."

CHAPTER TWENTY SEVEN

Not too many years ago, Duvall thought she might have actually enjoyed the rave. Though, seeing it up close and personal, she understood why Brett Alvarez had been so adamant that they weren't raves. There were no flashing lights, no tacky and repetitive techno music. As she stepped closer to the bonfire that served as the epicenter of the party, she took in the people. For the most part, none of them could really be stereotyped into one group or the other. She saw guys in both Under Armour shirts and ratty, basic t-shirts. She saw khakis and cargo shorts, Apple watches and hemp necklaces.

There were a few that did match the new-hippie details she'd heard of. Simple clothes, maybe a little dirty, and clearly high as a kite. She saw a group of eight people standing in a tight group, swaying to the music as if they were trees and a gentle wind was passing through them. The music itself was almost calming and, even though Duvall didn't quite like it, was sort of beautiful.

While it was a fairly easy group of people—so far about forty or so—to compartmentalize, it also made it hard to pick out who might be a killer. As she made her way through the crowd, she looked over to the right where a sleek, thin table was set up off in the shadows. She saw the faint blue and green glow of the dj set up. A man was behind the table, a large set of headphones covering the sides of his face and swaying like the people in the group she'd just seen.

That's where she spotted Brett Alvarez. He was standing with the dj, slightly off to the side. He was clearly spooked and off his game. It was irritating because the last thing she, Rachel, and Jack needed was for the organizer of this entire thing to look like he was waiting for the world to end. She almost went over to speak to him but figured that might seem even stranger to anyone that might be looking.

Not that there was anyone really looking in the direction of the dj. She could already see little groups starting to break away from the larger circuit of the party. As she meandered through the bodies, she saw a handful of people taking pills of some kind or another. Elsewhere, just out of the glow of the large bonfire, she saw several people setting up a little spot of their own. One was laying out a blanket while another was preparing a strange-looking pipe.

She did her best not to stare, trying to keep a clam look on her face. It was then that she realized that not many people were simply wandering around as if they were lost. She stopped and made something of an act of sitting down, doing so in a way that would make others think she didn't quite trust her legs. She sat down a good distance away from the light and heat of the fire, thinking there was no way a potential killer would approach her or anyone else so close to the party's only light source.

As she sat there, she closed her eyes just enough to allow her to still see; the hope was that the others would think she was zoned out or tripping while she was actually just keeping an eye on things. Everyone was polite as they walked around her. One woman that walked by even leaned down to run her fingers through Duvall's hair.

Duvall then lowered her head and spoke, barely opening her mouth to do so. "About fifty people. More coming in every few minutes. Chilled atmosphere. Lots of drugs."

She remained where she sat and was surprised when another woman sat down beside her. The woman was softly laughing under her breath, clearly high on something.

"This energy," the woman said. "This energy...I need to share it. Do you feel it?"

Duvall had no idea what to say to this, so she simply made a pleasing "*mmm*" sound. She rocked slightly, trying to play the part. And as she did, her eyes found a man that was only now starting to appear through the darkness on the other side of the fire. He stood out slightly because he was dressed in a black t-shirt and walked as if he were suspicious of everyone. His arms were covered in tattoos. A broken Celtic cross ran up the length of his right arm and on his left arm, a demon smiled from his shoulder, its tongue out and reaching down to the wrist. He looked rather grim, a storm cloud walking out in the midst of all of these pleasure-seeking partiers with their psychedelics and glow sticks.

She watched as he came directly over to them. His eyes wandered here and there, looking specifically at women. His right hand was in his pocket as he came around the fire. Duvall had a strange moment of uneasiness when she realized it seemed that the guy was coming right for her. This was going to be far too easy—if this was indeed their guy.

When he approached, she opened her eyes and looked up to him. He had black eye shadow around his eyes and another tattoo creeping up from under the collar of his shirt and reaching around to the back of his neck. He smiled down at them, his dark hair hanging low down over his brow.

"You ladies lonely?"

Duvall said nothing, only smiled at him uncertainly. The woman that had sat down beside her went rigid and looked up to the man as if he had kicked dirt in her face.

"Please don't bother my mood," the woman said, her tone like a teacher speaking to a disruptive child.

The man shot a look of absolute hatred in the woman's direction before softening his expression and looking at Duvall. He smirked with the sort of smile that showed the signs of a man that was usually quite good at speaking to women.

"And how about you?" he asked Duvall.

She thought about it for a moment. He'd been very blatant in terms of approaching her and from what she'd seen, he'd shown interest in only the women at the party as he'd walked her way. She had no idea if this was the killer or not, but she figured it would be best to speak with him a bit just in case rather than ignore him and find out when it was too late that he'd been right there in front of her, and she'd let him go.

"I don't know about the company," she said, slowly getting to her feet. She studied his face, trying to find a line somewhere between flirtatious and cautious. "Depends on what the company has to offer."

He smiled at her and took a step closer. The bonfire flickered on the left, the desert yawning its darkness to the right. "I've got something that will open your mind in more ways than you've ever dreamed of. Just two little hits and you'll break through like never before."

"That's what they all say."

He reached out and his fingers brushed the inside of her hand. He pressed a small bag into it. She clutched it and smiled. "How much?"

"Oh, it's free. It costs only your company."

She started to look at the bag, but he took her hand again, with force this time but still relatively soft. "Not here. Not yet. Let's walk off a ways. Would that be okay? It will be worth it. You can trust me."

"Yeah, okay," she said, her eyes locking with his.

She did not like what she saw there but knew that she'd taken the hook now. He took the tips of her fingers in his hand and pulled her away from the fire—away from the sure safety of the party and into the waiting dark.

***

"That's what they all say."

Rachel and Jack were sitting in Duvall's car when her voice came over the miniature radio, speaking these words. Jack shook his head and opened the door, peering out into the darkness, over near The Three Brothers.

"I know it wasn't the code word, but we need to at least get closer," he said. "She's about to engage."

Rachel, not typically the sort to upturn a plan that had already been set in place, couldn't help but agree. Things were happening faster than she'd expected and she wasn't about to let the case or Duvall's safety slip away so quickly.

"Okay, so we move in closer," she said. "Take the radio and keep the volume *low*. We can get closer, but we can't show up at the site yet."

She thought he was going to argue this but only gave her a nod. He removed the radio from its place on the dashboard and closed the car door. As they started hurrying away from the car and heading toward the glow of the bonfire slightly to the east, they heard the faint murmurs of the male voice coming through the radio.

"...walk off a ways. Would that be okay? It will be worth it. You can trust me."

And then, after a slight pause, Duvall's voice came again. *"Yeah, okay."*

"Jesus," Jack muttered.

They jogged as quietly as they could through the darkness. Rachel's eyes continued to give her problems, making the resolute darkness all the more treacherous. She followed closely behind Jack, making sure to follow along in his footsteps. The night was a blur of nothing around her. The only thing breaking it was the outline of Jack directly ahead of her and the growing glow of the fire roughly a quarter of a mile ahead.

Through the soft tumult of their steps, she could hear Duvall's voice from the radio, still held in Jack's right hand. *"Hey., I'm not trying to go on a desert hike in the middle of the night."*

"Just a bit further," the man replied. *"I don't want a lot of people seeing us. I don't have much to give out."*

"What is it, anyway?"

"You'll see."

The fire grew brighter, and the music was so close now that Rachel could barely hear the voices coming through the radio. She drew up closer to Jack, making sure she missed nothing. They were close enough to the party now that she could also just barely hear the chatter of people from the party.

"Okay, I think this should be good," the man said. *"So, you can take that now."*

"Not until you tell me what it is. Are you—"

"I said take the fucking thing."

There was the sound of movement, barely there at all over their footfalls and the increasing volume of the music. But what she heard next had both her and Jack forgetting about remaining quiet.

"Hey, let go of my wrist." And then, as if saying the word while drawing in a breath, she added a gasped: *"Ink pen."*

Jack let out grunt of frustration as he took off at full sprint. Rachel followed along behind him, running as quickly as her feet and faulty vision would allow.

CHAPTER TWENTY EIGHT

He'd been at this damn party for nearly half an hour now and hadn't seen Ashlyn yet. He'd plastered a picture of her in his mind, her full lips smiling at him in front of several rows of vinyl. Sure, he knew maybe she'd decided not to come but something about their interaction made him think she would be here.

Not only her, but the forces behind his ritual seemed to think so, too. They seemed to think she was going to be the one. The next one...and maybe the last one. After Ashlyn, maybe the ritual would finally be complete.

The music was the same, the people were the same, and the drugs were very much the same. Before leaving his house, he'd gone into his little supply and picked out a few different pills and a bag of mushroom caps. He wasn't sure which one he'd use tonight. Usually, he let the universe decide. He was, after all, only a moving vessel in it. That was, of course, until the ritual was complete, and he was immortal.

Not seeing Ashlyn, he knew he would have to find a backup. But it couldn't be just anyone. She had to be perfect—a perfect and fitting sacrifice. The first woman he saw was not worthy because she was beyond wasted; he could smell beer on her, already drunk and on the way to getting high as well. The second woman he saw was too short.

Ah, but the third woman...wait a second, she might do.

She was sitting on the ground with another woman. She sat almost completely still. Her mouth was open as she spoke quietly, whether to herself or her neighbor. They sat a good distance away from the fire, which was perfect for him.

But rather than go right to her, he waited. He had to watch. He had to make sure she was going to be the right choice.

She was very pretty, in a plain sort of way. There was a look of innocence about her, a surefire quality of a good, pure heart. Yes, she would do. he could feel it. He could feel the universe telling him that she would do just fine.

He started walking towards her but stopped when another man approached. He was dressed in a black shirt and had tattoos everywhere. Greasy black hair hung over his brow, and he smiled as he looked down at the pair of women.

Watching as the man spoke to his backup made him feel uneasy. Was he going to really fail tonight? Would the success of the ritual be delayed even longer?

Apparently so. While one of the women flat-out rejected the man with tattoos and black hair the woman he'd seen as his backup stood up with him. They spoke for a moment and then the man took her by the hand. They walked off into the darkness beyond the fire—as if the man was taking a page right out his playbook.

Fury built up within him for a moment, but he got a grip on it. The night was young. Even if Ashlyn did not show up, there were others. There would be more. He'd been to enough of these wretched things to know that some people didn't bother showing up until nearly two in the morning.

As usual, he found that his ability to stamp out emotions like frustration and anger paid off. He turned back to the fire, ready to start the hunt anew, when his eyes fell on her. Ashlyn had come after all. A smile stretched across his face as he stepped back into the shadows. He didn't want her to see him. Not yet.

The smile got even wider when he watched her pop something into her mouth and, with a slight expression of ecstasy, swallow it down. She was wearing a thin white shirt, no bra, and the same pants she'd been wearing at the record store.

She'd already taken something. It didn't matter what. He just needed to wait a few minutes and then he'd go up to her. And even if she was still with friends, they still had that connection from the record store. He was quite sure he would not have a problem getting her to come with him.

Still smiling, he looked up into the night sky and thanked whatever forces had designed this all. He'd been obedient and patient. He'd kept control of his emotions and the universe had delivered his ideal sacrifice right to him.

Yes, this would be the final night, the final sacrifice. He could feel it all lined up for him. He thought of the knife he'd planted out in the desert, of the rock he'd slid it under. It was just a smile away, a bit shy of the rock formation known as The Three Brothers—a fitting altar if there ever was one.

He waited, his hands getting clammy, and he watched. When he saw the familiar glaze in her eyes and the tension in her unsteady legs, he made his way over to her. And when they locked eyes and a smile of recognition filled her face, he knew he had her. The hard part was over and now the only thing left was one more heart to take.

And beyond that, immortality.

CHAPTER TWENTY NINE

Rachel had no doubt that Duvall could handle herself. She could certainly handle herself long enough for her and Jack to come to her aid. Still, the sound of a skirmish coming through the radio Jack still held was unnerving. She heard Duvall cry out a single time, and then a surprised yelp from the man that had led her off into the darkness.

They were very close now. The fire was so close that Rachel could see the shapes of partygoers around it. A little farther to her right, she could see the shape of The Three Brothers in the distance. If they got any closer, the people at the party would see them racing through the night, as if being chased by some great monster of the desert.

So then where the hell are Duvall and her attacker?

She couldn't see them anywhere. But then again, anything outside of that orange-yellow glow to her right was little more than a blur. Even the sheet of darkness that was the night seemed to blur in places.

"Shit," Jack said. "I don't see anything!"

Rachel made the mistake of glancing all around, looking for any sort of movement in the darkness. She couldn't even see Jack anymore. She opened her mouth to call for him but before she could say anything, her foot struck something—a rock or just hard scrub grass, she wasn't sure. She went sprawling forward, nearly catching her balance, but ultimately falling.

It was a gentle fall, and she was able to catch herself fairly well on her hands. She was more embarrassed than anything else and, for the first time, was grateful it was dark.

This tumor is going to kill you before it actually *kills you,* she thought. *What the hell are you doing running in the darkness with just one good eye?*

She knew it was a logical thought, but she pushed it aside as she got back to her feet. Rachel took a moment, looking around for any sign of Jack. She didn't see him anywhere, and she sure as hell couldn't call out for him and give their position away. So, with no other alternative, she continued running forward. Knowing that Jack was no longer in front of her, she felt totally alone, like she could very well be the only woman on the face of the planet. The illusion was shattered by the thumping and ambient tones of the music from her right, though.

She looked out that way and *thought* she saw a dark shape about twenty feet ahead of her, a single form in the darkness against the glow of the fire. Jack…maybe. She could—

But then she heard a slight commotion from directly ahead. She continued running forward, dong her very best to see through the darkness. Finally, she did see moving shapes ahead in the dark, murky movement that she was quickly closing in on.

She heard a man groan, followed by a female's low-throated complaint.

"Duvall?" she said into the darkness, slowing her pace.

"Yeah. I'm here. I'm good. I got the bastard."

Rachel started forward, fumbling for her phone in her pocket. She grabbed it and cut the flashlight on. What she saw didn't really surprise her and she suddenly felt foolish for having run so fast through the desert, thinking she was going to be Duvall's savior.

Duvall was perched on top of a man. He looked to be in his mid-twenties, his arms decked out in tattoos and his hair a dirty, black mop on top of his head. Duvall had cuffed the man, his arms pulled behind his back. She had a knee in his back and scowl on her face.

As Rachel hurried over, she saw something else. There was a small knife on the desert floor—not even a knife, really, but more like utility knife. Something about this alarmed Rachel…it didn't quite add up.

"Duvall? What happened?"

"He tried to force two pills down my throat," she said, getting to her feet. "And when I wouldn't take them, he grabbed my wrist and then my breasts. He tried to force me down to the ground, instantly going for the button on my pants. And then I monkey-flipped the asshole."

"You're okay?"

"Yeah, just pissed off."

"Duvall, the knife he had…"

"Yeah, I know. It's not right, is it? This guy…"

It's not our guy, Rachel thought, her stomach churning. "Jack didn't come through?"

"No. Haven't seen him."

'He was running off to—"

Her phone buzzed in her hand as the flashlight continued to shine down on Duvall and her recent arrest. She killed the light and turned the phone to her face. She was confused to see it was Jack. He must have really gotten turned around out in the dark—or had maybe seen something that led him further away from her and Duvall.

She answered it, wasting no time. "I found Duvall. The guy isn't what we're looking for, Duvall's okay. She got—"

"Okay, then if he's not our guy, you need to get over here. I'm at the party...and we've got something of a situation."

***

Rachel and Duvall made their way over to the bonfire. The music was still going but the chatter was dying down. It was little more than a murmur when they arrived but when people saw them quickly escorting a handcuffed man along, it went dead still. People started hurrying off into the darkness, but Rachel stopped them before anyone could make it very far.

"Nope," she said. "No one moves. There are three FBI agents here and if you try running off, we're going to assume you're taking part in a case we're working. Don't move. We're not interested in what you're doing out here. Stay still and *don't interfere*. And dj...don't stop the music. Everything has to remain as close to the same as possible."

The dj nodded, though it was clear he was very uncomfortable. A thick tension fell over the crowd as Rachel and Duvall hurried over to Jack. He was standing beside a tall girl wearing nothing but a bikini. She was crying and trembling slightly.

"She can't find her friend," Jack said. "She says her friend was right here one minute and gone the next. She could be overreacting because even she'll admit that she's tripping her ass off. But she says it's not right...not like her friend."

"What's her name?"

The tall girl looked to Rachel with shining eyes—a result of both the high and fresh tears. "Ashlyn. She...she was *right there.*"

Rachel looked to Duvall and Jack. The tattooed man, still in cuffs, had settled down onto the ground, his head hung in defeat. "We need to fan out. Duvall, do you mind calling the squads that are on standby? Tell them the situation—that we might have a manhunt on our hands within the next five minutes."

"Got it. I'll take this way," she said, nodding straight ahead.

"I'll go back around the opposite way," Jack said, nodding to the other side of the bonfire.

"And I'll head over here," Rachel said, already starting toward the majestic silhouettes of The Three Brothers.

As he turned and headed for the rock formation straight out ahead of them, she watched Duvall lug the tattooed man over to the dj table, uncuffing him long enough to then cuff him again—one cuff on his wrist, the other on one of the metal table legs. Everyone watched, some with sober eyes and other with befuddled stoned ones. It was easily one of the oddest moments of her career—made even stranger by the fact that she was about to rush back into the darkness with only one good eye to guide her.

As she ran, Rachel heard Jack next to her, fanning out to the left and putting more distance between them. She felt the music behind her, the bass of it seeming to push her along. She recalled easily tripping and falling less than ten minutes ago and did her best to be more careful this time. Slowly, the glow of the fire waned and she was facing pure darkness. It was almost dizzying; the only thing anchoring her were the shapes of those three rocks up ahead.

A trio of rocks that, in her opinion, would make a pretty decent altar setting.

As if summoned by that thought, she suddenly heard a shout from directly ahead of her. It was a shout of pain, followed by something that was almost like a gasp, a sound that was barely there but had just enough pain in it to carry up into the air a bit.

Rachel drew her sidearm, her body seeming to track the direction of the sounds. The shapes appeared out of the darkness slowly but when they did, they were all too familiar. The shape of one person was falling on top of a form on the ground. As her eyes focused on the shapes, her one good eye seemed to adjust better to the darkness.

The man perching over the figure on the ground had a knife in his hand. A very large knife, streaked with blood.

"Stop right there!" she shouted, stopping to take a shooter's stance. Her feet skidding on the hardp dirt but her knees locked, keeping her upright.

The man let out a frustrated growl and rocketed off of the body. He ran hard to the right, trying to veil himself in the darkness. For the most part, it worked. She tried tracking him, but the motion against the darkness and her faulty vision made it next to impossible to follow his progress.

"Jack!" she screamed. "He's coming your way."

She kept her gun out in the direction she thought the man had gone as she sidestepped over to the fallen body. As she'd expected, it was a girl. The man had stabbed her in the stomach a single time. It also appeared as if he'd already started working on getting her undressed.

"Ashlyn?" she said.

The woman was breathing hard, squirming on her back. Rachel looked down to her, trying to gauge the severity of the wound. "We've got cops on the way. Hang in there, Ashlyn, and you'll be—"

She caught motion out of the corner of her right eye, but it was far too late. She turned just in time to see the knife coming towards her neck. She tried to sidestep and was mostly successful. Rather than tearing through her neck, the blade clipped her inner shoulder. She felt the skin shred open, and the blade bounce off of her collarbone. She wheeled around, throwing a hard punch into the darkness. It landed on what felt like the back of the man's head but by that time, he was already on her.

His weight pushed her to the ground, his free hand punching hard against the area he'd just cut open. Rachel screamed, willing herself not to let go of her gun. But when she hit the ground, the wind went rushing out of her and her hand opened up just enough to release it.

Her scream was cut off abruptly as she couldn't draw in a breath. And then the man was on her, raising the knife. She heard the music behind them and thought of the rituals Professor Paddock had mentioned, the Aztecs carrying out this same thing as a crowd watched on. She tried to fight back, but she was too overpowered.

The knife came down and all Rachel could do was raise her hands, hoping it was enough to block a deathblow.

CHAPTER THIRTY

Rachel had come close to death a few times during the course of her career, but she'd never actually thought she was going to die. Yet as the killer drove the knife down, she had to come to terms with it. And there was a small, morbid part within her that couldn't help but think: *well, at least the tumor won't be what does you in.*

The gunshot that sounded out seemed to obliterate that thought. It also caused the killer to snap hard to the left, falling off of her. The night and her clouded vision may have been playing tricks on her, but she was pretty sure the blade had been less than six inches from slamming into her breastbone. She gasped for breath as she scrambled to her feet, her eyes tracing back and forth between the fallen killer and the darkness.

Jack came hurrying over to her, gun drawn, his eyes still on the killer. He stopped at Rachel and her heart broke a little when she saw that he was on the verge of tears. "Are you okay?"

"Yeah. He got me in shoulder. It hurts like hell."

"Okay. Stay here."

He got up and walked slowly to the killer. Rachel watched as the man writhed on the ground. She couldn't see where Jack had shot the man but if Jack had gone by bureau protocol, it had been high in the shoulder. Meanwhile, the stab victim continued to breathe in harsh, quick gasps just a few yards away.

"What's your name?" Jack asked the killer.

"You...you can't stop me. I'm in the middle of something very important."

"I am, too, asshole. What's your name?"

"I'm going to be immortal," the man said with a sick chuckle. "I may already be."

"If you keep talking, we might just find out."

"You...you..."

The killer rolled over quickly, screaming as he did so. He threw something at Jack—something that made no sense to Rachel at first. It looked like a strange little cloud in the darkness. It wasn't until Jack grunted in surprise and took a single, stumbling step back that Rachel understood that the killer had thrown dirt from the desert floor into Jack's face.

It was a minor attack, but it did the job. The killer lashed out with his knife. The blade caught Jack high on the shin. The killer then came surging forward just as Jack brought his gun back down. The killer slashed out again, this time cutting Jack across the back of the hand. His hand opened reflexively and his gun fell to the ground.

As Rachel got to her knees, she noticed far too many things at once. First, she noticed that the vision in her right eye was completely gone again. Second, she saw Duvall racing in their direction, her sidearm also drawn. And then there was the third thing—a clarity that came hard over her and chilled her to the core.

Immortality. He was taking the hearts in a bid to win immortality from some god—perhaps the very same Sun God that Paddock had told her about.

"You're here for immortality?" she asked, taking one last shot at this. She'd much rather arrest the man and have him go to trial than simply kill him. Maybe she could sway him. Maybe she could get into his head.

"I am," he said. The question seemed to have stopped him, making his entire body respond in a way that now seemed almost calm and reverent.

"I am, too. And I thought it would be here. I...I have a tumor. Inoperable. One year left. I need...I need you to show me."

"No. It's only for me. You have to do the work."

And with that, he charged her.

She was going to have to kill this man. No battle, no arrest. She was going to have to kill him.

She fumbled along the desert floor for her Glock, never taking her good eye off of the man as he drew the knife back again, almost like a javelin.

Rachel brought her gun up and aimed as well as she could with her left eye, peering into the darkness. She held her breath, focused, and fired.

The shot took the man in the chest, dead center. He rocked back, falling to his knees and screaming. *"Sacri...fice...almost done...you...you CAN'T..."*

And then, somehow, he got to his feet and started for her again. He still clasped the knife as he came for her. Wincing, Rachel fired again. The shot landed about an inch from her last shot, nearly in his heart.

Again, he stumbled back but he would not fall. He opened his mouth to say something, but no sound came out.

But he smiled.

Jesus, he wants to be immortal, Rachel thought. *Did he...did he manage to do it? Did he...*

Before she realized how dumb that thought was, he took another step toward her. He was ten feet away from her now. Behind him, Jack watched on, stupefied. Duvall was to the man's right, perched in a shooter's stance with an astonished look on her face.

The man took another step. Rachel nearly squeezed off a third shot—which would be the fourth shot the man had taken—when he finally gave in. He fell to his knees and glanced back to the fallen girl, the girl named Ashlyn.

"I hear them singing," the man said, his voice haggard. Blood started trickling from his mouth. He tried a single time to get back to his feet but could not push himself up. "Singing...the hearts. A chorus...they were so happy...singing...can live forever..."

Something like laughter came out of his throat as he bled onto the desert floor.

Rachel felt something loosen inside of her. She shook her head against it, as if trying to ward it off. But in the end, it came and it came hard. She dropped her gun to the ground, turned away from Jack and Duvall, and began to cry.

The music continued to blare from down below them and she hoped it drowned out her sobs as Jack and Duvall checked on Ashlyn and the killer. She heard Duvall calling 911 for an ambulance as she turned her attention to the sky. Up above a canopy of stars hid away a heaven that seemed to almost suggest the reality of something like immortality but, at the end of the day, offered only a cruel imitation of it at best.

CHAPTER THIRTY ONE

Rachel sipped from a paper cup of green tea, watching the wall-mounted television in her hospital room. It was 6:05 in the morning and the local morning news was exploding with the events that had transpired out in the desert. She watched as a newscaster stood in front of The Three Brothers, describing the scene that had taken place on the other side of the rock formation just five hours ago.

Rachel knew what had happened all too well. She'd sat in the desert for exactly seventeen minutes before the first ambulance arrived. It had come across the desert floor, coming in off of the access road that led to the scenic view for The Three Brothers. One thing the newscaster mentioned in an almost casual way was that somehow, so far, no one had died. Rachel chewed on that for a moment, finding it miraculous.

Her own injury had been somewhat minimal. The cut along her collarbone had indeed gone down to the bone. The wound required twenty-two stitches and orders from the doctor not to do anything too strenuous with the arm anytime soon. She'd been given a shot for the pain before the stitches and had dozed off. When she woke up at 5:40, the stitches had been put in and she was no worse for the wear.

Jack was in the same boat. Neither of his cuts had required stitches, but the one to the back of his hand had come in at such an angle that the entire thing was wrapped in gauze. The dressing nearly made it look like he'd broken his hand.

As she watched the news, telling the story of a man named Edgar Denbrook, Jack came into her room. He had two muffins from the cafeteria, setting them down on the bedside table. Without a word between them, Rachel chose banana nut as she listened to the newscaster. Edgar Denbrook had been apprehended not too far away from the rock formation, on the cusp of claiming his fourth victim. That victim, a twenty-four-year-old woman named Ashlyn Myers was currently in intensive care, still alive but with a fight ahead of her. The same was true of Edgar Denbrook. He'd been shot three times but, upon leaving the scene, had still been alive.

"And he still is," Jack said, taking the remaining muffin—blueberry—with his left hand. "I just checked with one of the people at the front desk. Used my bureau clout. Edgar Denbrook came out of surgery forty minutes ago. He's going to spend quite a bit of time in the hospital due to a nicked lung, but he'll likely survive."

"And then spend the rest of his life in prison," Rachel said. "That's what I have to keep telling myself."

She wanted to say something else. She wanted to say that his muttering about immortality had spooked her, mainly because the son of a bitch simply would not fall. And the fact that he was coming out of this alive at all was sort of miraculous. Her last shot had been from close range and had been very close to his heart.

She wiped the thought out of her mind and looked back to Jack. Her right eye was back to working at a lazy rate. She was starting to almost prefer the stupid thing to be totally blank and useless. The constant blur reminded her of what was wrong with her. She'd nearly mentioned it when she'd had to tell the doctors about her tumor when she'd been checked in. But she wasn't about to have the end of this case marred with yet another of her issues. With the case now closed, she just wanted to get home. It turned out she had told Paige the truth; it was looking like she *would* be home by tomorrow night.

"We were lucky, you know?" Jack asked. "Saving the girl, I mean—and not getting too badly hurt."

"Speak for yourself. My shoulder is a bitch."

"Well, you know what I mean."

"I do."

As they both looked back up to the television, where the news anchor was now on to another story, the door to the room opened again. This time it was Duvall that entered. She was carrying two tacky mylar balloons, both reading GET WELL SOON. Rachel couldn't help but laugh.

"I know, I know," Duvall said. "But I wasn't sure what the appropriate gift was for two people that just stopped a murderer. Balloons seemed much more appropriate than one of those fruit bouquets."

"Did you get things squared away with your supervisor?" Jack asked.

"A bit. There's a meeting tomorrow for the official debrief. And I feel like I owe you two an enormous degree of thanks. Hence the balloons."

"Thanks for what?" Rachel said.

"Lester is officially in custody for the murder of Simone Switzer. The guy that tried to assault me turned out to be a serial rapist out of California, and I played a part in the capture of a guy that was cutting hearts out of women in the desert. I know it sounds selfish, but this thing is making me look like gold. And that's not my talking...those were words straight out of my supervisor's mouth."

"Looks like your future is pretty bright," Jack said, practically beaming at her.

"It will be. The hard stuff needs to be covered first. I got a call about ten minutes ago, while I was waiting for the gift shop to open. A team of agents and cops working together ransacked Edgar Denbrook's house. They found a hidden room with weird symbols all over it—some Satanic in nature and some that seem to have Aztec origins. Just a whole weird mess of stuff. And in that room, they found three hearts. Of course, DNA tests will have to be performed, but I'm as sure as you two are that they'll belong to our victims."

"Duvall," Rachel said, not quite sure why she was getting teary-eyed. "Thanks for all of your help. The good stuff that *does* come your way after this...you deserve all of it."

Duvall flushed a bit, her cheeks getting red. "Well," she said, doing her best to hide the emotion that was coming to the surface, "I'll leave you two to heal. It was a pleasure working with you. And if you find yourself out this way again, don't hesitate to call."

She took turns shaking their hands, lingering just a bit longer when she offered her hand to Jack. She looked as if she wanted to say something else but simply turned to the door. On her way out, she turned one more time and waved to them as the door closed.

The room was silent for just a moment. Rachel sighed and looked at Jack. She felt awful for being so irritated and indifferent to whatever had been evolving between them. Apparently, a brush with death had shifted her perspective on things.

"How's your hand feeling?" she asked.

"It hurts a little. Not too bad."

"Good. But if you don't get your ass out there right now and talk to her—even if it's just to exchange phone numbers—I'm going to cut you. And it'll be much worse than the little flesh wound on your hands."

Jack laughed and started to shake his head. But at the last moment, he looked at the door and smiled. "Yeah. I don't want to get cut again. I'll be right back."

"Take your time," she called to him as he made his way to the door.

When the door closed behind him, she found herself alone again. She turned the TV off and sat in silence. She rested her head back, wanting to go to sleep but knowing she couldn't. She was too wound up, her mind too active. It was more than just having closed the case, though. She was more preoccupied with how she was supposed to tell Paige that she was dying.

Compared to that heartbreaking task, she thought the last few days might seem almost like a tiny little paradise.

CHAPTER THIRTY TWO

Even after Rachel returned home to Richmond, Grandma Tate stayed around for another day. She then left and went back home to Aiken, South Carolina, with plans to come back in a week. Rachel spent that week with Paige completely work free as her stitches healed up. They watched movies and ate junk food on the couch. She allowed Paige to skip two days of school so that they could play putt-putt (which was harder on her shoulder than she'd anticipated) and visit a horse and pony farm out in the Chesterfield area.

As it was all happening, it seemed to be the very thing Rachel needed—uninterrupted time with her daughter. On the single occasion Peter had called her, she'd explained things to him as best as she could without getting into an argument. She was going to tell their daughter that she was dying, and she wanted to spend a week of Mommy-Daughter time together beforehand. And no, she did not want him there when she told her.

She did, however, take Grandma Tate up on that very kind offer. They set the plan together just before Grandma Tate left. The first afternoon on her return visit, the three of them would sit down in the living room and it would all come out.

That how it came to be that Grandma Tate was once again back in the Gift living room, looking over at Paige and Rachel with a look of sadness. Paige, who had just been called into the room, looked at both of them with apprehension. She knew something was wrong…she just didn't know what.

"Paige," Rachel said, "I wanted to talk to you about something very important. And I hate to keep throwing things at you because I know you've been through a lot—with things going bad between your dad and I, with Grandma Tate's sickness. But you've been such a brave little girl and I hope you can stay brave with this new thing I need to tell you."

"Something…something else bad?"

Rachel could only nod for a moment. She found it ironic that she could talk to grieving parents about how their child has just been found dead, but this…this was infinitely worse for some reason.

"Yeah, I'm afraid so. Um...so, you know how Grandma Tate is sick, right?"

"Yeah. With cancer. But she *might* be okay if she keeps going to the doctor."

"That's right. But the thing is, there are all sorts of different kinds of cancer. Sometimes it comes in the form of a thing called a tumor. Sometimes tumors can grow on people's hearts, or anywhere in the body, really. Sometimes they even show up on people's brains."

"Okay..."

The girl was terrified, her eyes going glassy. Seeing her like that, Rachel knew she had to just go ahead and rip the band-aid off.

"A few months ago, I went to the doctor because I passed out at work. And when I was there, the doctor...well, he found one of those tumors. He found one on my brain."

"Yeah, well are you okay?"

"Right now, I do feel fine. So that's great. But the thing is, that over time, I—"

Paige started shaking her head. She also started kneading at her hair, a nervous tick she'd had ever since her hair had been long enough to do so. "Mommy....are you going to die?"

"Probably. Again, I feel fine now, and I want to cherish the time I have left with you. But according to the doctors, there's not much of a chance for me."

"But there *is* a chance, right?"

She thought of the special treatment she'd been offered—the treatment that sounded a little scary and really offered only the tiniest little sliver of hope.

"Well, there—"

"No!" She screamed it like a child that had just been spooked by a movie. "You go to the doctors and you let them fix it! You can't...Mommy...you..."

But her voice cracked, then broke, and she was wailing. Rachel ran to her and took her daughter in her arms. She hugged her tight as Paige cried against her recently stitched shoulder. When Rachel started crying, doing everything she could to keep it as quiet as possible, Grandma Tate also came over and joined in on the hug.

Three generations of women sat on the couch in an awkward hug, crying over deaths that had not yet come to claim their due. It was heart wrenching but there was also a comfort in it that took Rachel by surprise. She knew that for Paige to have any semblance of a normal life, she was going to have to try patching things up with Peter. Paige was going to need both of her parents to help her in a phase of life where she'd only have one.

But for the meantime, she simply held her daughter close. She thought of those women in the desert, their chests opened up and their hearts taken away. Right now, they both had their hearts. They both had their hearts and the blood pumping through them. And together on the couch, all three of them embracing, that seemed like the only thing that really mattered.

* * *

Rachel sat down at the kitchen table and placed a bottle of bourbon in front of Grandma Tate's mug of coffee. She then took the seat across from her with her own cup. It was decaf, though. It was ten o' clock at night and it was far too late for caffeine when she was not on a case. She looked at the coffee cups and the bourbon, pleased to see that tonight, her right eye seemed to be operating almost at full capacity.

"She finally asleep?" Grandma Tate asked.

"Yeah. She stopped crying finally, and I just held her until she fell asleep."

"She's a resilient kid. She'll come around to it. It will be hard as hell, but she will come around. You on the other hand...I won't presume to tell you how to live your life, but you need to go to the doctor. Even if it's just to keep her mind at ease, you have to."

"I know."

"And there's another reason I'd really like for you to at least give it a try."

"What's that?"

Grandma Tate got up from the table and walked to the bar, where her purse hung from the back of one of the stools. She reached inside and took out several folded sheets of papers. She handed them to Rachel and then took her seat back.

"What is this?" Rachel asked.

"Read it."

Rachel opened up the papers, terrified it was another note from Alex Lynch. She glanced them over, quickly realizing it was not anything from Lynch as Grandma Tate added a splash of bourbon to her coffee.

She was looking at a doctor's report. Some sort of lab results that went way over her head. "I'm still lost," she said.

"I didn't want to throw too much stuff at Paige earlier. But those are my latest lab results. Bloodwork, the whole kit and kaboodle. My doctors don't understand it and I sure as hell don't understand it, but I've gone into remission."

"Ae you...what? Are they sure?"

"They are. They're absolutely baffled but they *are* sure. One of my specialists said it was a miracle. A doctor *actually* used that word. Now, they want me back next week to run some more tests just to be absolutely certain but based on what you have in your hands...yeah. I'm beating it. Which is odd because I've not really started any treatments yet."

A very peculiar feeling raced through Rachel. Was it envy? Jealousy? Or was it something a bit darker? Maybe it was a sense of this whole situation not being fair. Apparently, there were a lot of dark things popping up in light of facing a quickly approaching death.

"Oh my God," she said, staring at the papers. "This is...this is *incredible!*"

"I almost feel bad for telling you after what you went through, but I wanted to share it with you. I had to share it with *someone*. I just...I don't know how to take it. I don't buy into miracles, you know."

"So what does this mean? What does—"

She was interrupted by a very soft knocking on her front door. She got up from the table, curious as to who it might be. She figured it was probably Peter, deciding to come over to check on her after the talk with Paige. But in the back of her mind, she thought of Alex Lynch sending someone to her house to put that dead squirrel in Paige's room.

Quickly, she stood on her tiptoes and looked out of the bottom of three rectangular glass slats at the top of the door. It wasn't Peter, but another familiar face. Confused and rather relieved, she saw Jack on the other side. She hadn't seen him since they'd come back from New Mexico, but she *had* texted him to let him know she wasn't going to be in to work for a while. What she hadn't told him, though, was that even then, she planned to talk to Director Anderson about her situation.

She opened the door with a smile on her face. It was good to see him, after all, and she hadn't had the opportunity to tease him about Duvall a single time since they'd returned.

"Hey, Jack," she said. "What are you doing here so late?"

"Can I come in?"

"Of course."

And even as she said that, she noticed his stone-faced look. He looked grim and almost sad about something. He looked devastated.

"Jack? What is it?"

"Um...listen, Rachel...I got a call about half an hour ago. Straight from Anderson. I was going to just call, but I figured you should hear this face-to-face from me."

"Jesus, Jack. You're scaring me. What is it?"

"Well, it started as rumors, I think, but it was confirmed about two hours ago. The news came straight from the prison and—"

"Jack. What is it?"

He took a deep breath and when he looked her in the eyes, her heart deflated a bit. It then sank into some deep, dark pit inside of her when he answered.

"We don't know how yet, but Alex Lynch has somehow escaped from prison."

NOW AVAILABLE!

HER LAST CHOICE
(A Rachel Gift FBI Suspense Thriller —Book 5)

Patients at an end-of-life foundation are turning up dead—but not because of their illnesses. In a case that hits far too close to home, Rachel must race to discover who would rob the victims of their last days on earth—and why.

FBI Special Agent Rachel Gift is among the FBI's most brilliant agents at hunting down serial killers. She plans on doing this forever—until she discovers she has months left to live. Determined to go down fighting, and to keep her diagnosis a secret, Rachel faces her own mortality while trying to save other's lives. But how long can she go until she collapses under the weight of it all?

"A MASTERPIECE OF THRILLER AND MYSTERY.. Blake Pierce did a magnificent job developing characters with a psychological side so well described that we feel inside their minds, follow their fears and cheer for their success. Full of twists, this book will keep you awake until the turn of the last page."
--Books and Movie Reviews, Roberto Mattos (re Once Gone)

HER LAST CHOICE (A Rachel Gift FBI Suspense Thriller) is book #5 in a long-anticipated new series by #1 bestseller and USA Today bestselling author Blake Pierce, whose bestseller Once Gone (a free download) has received over 1,000 five star reviews.

FBI Agent Rachel Gift, 33, unparalleled for her ability to enter the minds of serial killers, is a rising star in the Behavioral Crimes Unit—until a routine doctor visit reveals she has but a few months left to live.

Not wishing to burden others with her pain, Rachel decides, agonizing as it is, not to tell anyone—not even her boss, her partner, her husband, or her seven-year-old daughter. She wants to go down fighting, and to take as many serial killers with her as she can.

In an ironic twist of fate, Rachel finds herself at an end-of-life charity, hunting down a killer more twisted than any she's seen yet.

Battling to push down her own complex emotions, Rachel must race against the clock to save the foundation's patients before the murderer strikes again.

A riveting and chilling crime thriller featuring a brilliant and flailing FBI agent, the RACHEL GIFT series is an unputdownable mystery, packed with suspense, twists and shocking secrets, propelled by a page-turning pace that will keep you bleary-eyed late into the night.

Book #6 in the series—HER LAST BREATH—is now also available!

Blake Pierce

Blake Pierce is the USA Today bestselling author of the RILEY PAGE mystery series, which includes seventeen books. Blake Pierce is also the author of the MACKENZIE WHITE mystery series, comprising fourteen books; of the AVERY BLACK mystery series, comprising six books; of the KERI LOCKE mystery series, comprising five books; of the MAKING OF RILEY PAIGE mystery series, comprising six books; of the KATE WISE mystery series, comprising seven books; of the CHLOE FINE psychological suspense mystery, comprising six books; of the JESSE HUNT psychological suspense thriller series, comprising twenty four books; of the AU PAIR psychological suspense thriller series, comprising three books; of the ZOE PRIME mystery series, comprising six books; of the ADELE SHARP mystery series, comprising fifteen books, of the EUROPEAN VOYAGE cozy mystery series, comprising four books; of the new LAURA FROST FBI suspense thriller, comprising nine books (and counting); of the new ELLA DARK FBI suspense thriller, comprising eleven books (and counting); of the A YEAR IN EUROPE cozy mystery series, comprising nine books, of the AVA GOLD mystery series, comprising six books (and counting); of the RACHEL GIFT mystery series, comprising six books (and counting); of the VALERIE LAW mystery series, comprising six books (and counting); and of the PAIGE KING mystery series, comprising six books (and counting).

An avid reader and lifelong fan of the mystery and thriller genres, Blake loves to hear from you, so please feel free to visit www.blakepierceauthor.com to learn more and stay in touch.

BOOKS BY BLAKE PIERCE

PAIGE KING MYSTERY SERIES
THE GIRL HE PINED (Book #1)
THE GIRL HE CHOSE (Book #2)
THE GIRL HE TOOK (Book #3)
THE GIRL HE WISHED (Book #4)
THE GIRL HE CROWNED (Book #5)
THE GIRL HE WATCHED (Book #6)

VALERIE LAW MYSTERY SERIES
NO MERCY (Book #1)
NO PITY (Book #2)
NO FEAR (Book #3)
NO SLEEP (Book #4)
NO QUARTER (Book #5)
NO CHANCE (Book #6)

RACHEL GIFT MYSTERY SERIES
HER LAST WISH (Book #1)
HER LAST CHANCE (Book #2)
HER LAST HOPE (Book #3)
HER LAST FEAR (Book #4)
HER LAST CHOICE (Book #5)
HER LAST BREATH (Book #6)

AVA GOLD MYSTERY SERIES
CITY OF PREY (Book #1)
CITY OF FEAR (Book #2)
CITY OF BONES (Book #3)
CITY OF GHOSTS (Book #4)
CITY OF DEATH (Book #5)
CITY OF VICE (Book #6)

A YEAR IN EUROPE
A MURDER IN PARIS (Book #1)
DEATH IN FLORENCE (Book #2)
VENGEANCE IN VIENNA (Book #3)

A FATALITY IN SPAIN (Book #4)

ELLA DARK FBI SUSPENSE THRILLER
GIRL, ALONE (Book #1)
GIRL, TAKEN (Book #2)
GIRL, HUNTED (Book #3)
GIRL, SILENCED (Book #4)
GIRL, VANISHED (Book 5)
GIRL ERASED (Book #6)
GIRL, FORSAKEN (Book #7)
GIRL, TRAPPED (Book #8)
GIRL, EXPENDABLE (Book #9)
GIRL, ESCAPED (Book #10)
GIRL, HIS (Book #11)

LAURA FROST FBI SUSPENSE THRILLER
ALREADY GONE (Book #1)
ALREADY SEEN (Book #2)
ALREADY TRAPPED (Book #3)
ALREADY MISSING (Book #4)
ALREADY DEAD (Book #5)
ALREADY TAKEN (Book #6)
ALREADY CHOSEN (Book #7)
ALREADY LOST (Book #8)
ALREADY HIS (Book #9)

EUROPEAN VOYAGE COZY MYSTERY SERIES
MURDER (AND BAKLAVA) (Book #1)
DEATH (AND APPLE STRUDEL) (Book #2)
CRIME (AND LAGER) (Book #3)
MISFORTUNE (AND GOUDA) (Book #4)
CALAMITY (AND A DANISH) (Book #5)
MAYHEM (AND HERRING) (Book #6)

ADELE SHARP MYSTERY SERIES
LEFT TO DIE (Book #1)
LEFT TO RUN (Book #2)
LEFT TO HIDE (Book #3)
LEFT TO KILL (Book #4)
LEFT TO MURDER (Book #5)

LEFT TO ENVY (Book #6)
LEFT TO LAPSE (Book #7)
LEFT TO VANISH (Book #8)
LEFT TO HUNT (Book #9)
LEFT TO FEAR (Book #10)
LEFT TO PREY (Book #11)
LEFT TO LURE (Book #12)
LEFT TO CRAVE (Book #13)
LEFT TO LOATHE (Book #14)
LEFT TO HARM (Book #15)

THE AU PAIR SERIES
ALMOST GONE (Book#1)
ALMOST LOST (Book #2)
ALMOST DEAD (Book #3)

ZOE PRIME MYSTERY SERIES
FACE OF DEATH (Book#1)
FACE OF MURDER (Book #2)
FACE OF FEAR (Book #3)
FACE OF MADNESS (Book #4)
FACE OF FURY (Book #5)
FACE OF DARKNESS (Book #6)

A JESSIE HUNT PSYCHOLOGICAL SUSPENSE SERIES
THE PERFECT WIFE (Book #1)
THE PERFECT BLOCK (Book #2)
THE PERFECT HOUSE (Book #3)
THE PERFECT SMILE (Book #4)
THE PERFECT LIE (Book #5)
THE PERFECT LOOK (Book #6)
THE PERFECT AFFAIR (Book #7)
THE PERFECT ALIBI (Book #8)
THE PERFECT NEIGHBOR (Book #9)
THE PERFECT DISGUISE (Book #10)
THE PERFECT SECRET (Book #11)
THE PERFECT FAÇADE (Book #12)
THE PERFECT IMPRESSION (Book #13)
THE PERFECT DECEIT (Book #14)
THE PERFECT MISTRESS (Book #15)

THE PERFECT IMAGE (Book #16)
THE PERFECT VEIL (Book #17)
THE PERFECT INDISCRETION (Book #18)
THE PERFECT RUMOR (Book #19)
THE PERFECT COUPLE (Book #20)
THE PERFECT MURDER (Book #21)
THE PERFECT HUSBAND (Book #22)
THE PERFECT SCANDAL (Book #23)
THE PERFECT MASK (Book #24)

CHLOE FINE PSYCHOLOGICAL SUSPENSE SERIES
NEXT DOOR (Book #1)
A NEIGHBOR'S LIE (Book #2)
CUL DE SAC (Book #3)
SILENT NEIGHBOR (Book #4)
HOMECOMING (Book #5)
TINTED WINDOWS (Book #6)

KATE WISE MYSTERY SERIES
IF SHE KNEW (Book #1)
IF SHE SAW (Book #2)
IF SHE RAN (Book #3)
IF SHE HID (Book #4)
IF SHE FLED (Book #5)
IF SHE FEARED (Book #6)
IF SHE HEARD (Book #7)

THE MAKING OF RILEY PAIGE SERIES
WATCHING (Book #1)
WAITING (Book #2)
LURING (Book #3)
TAKING (Book #4)
STALKING (Book #5)
KILLING (Book #6)

RILEY PAIGE MYSTERY SERIES
ONCE GONE (Book #1)
ONCE TAKEN (Book #2)
ONCE CRAVED (Book #3)

ONCE LURED (Book #4)
ONCE HUNTED (Book #5)
ONCE PINED (Book #6)
ONCE FORSAKEN (Book #7)
ONCE COLD (Book #8)
ONCE STALKED (Book #9)
ONCE LOST (Book #10)
ONCE BURIED (Book #11)
ONCE BOUND (Book #12)
ONCE TRAPPED (Book #13)
ONCE DORMANT (Book #14)
ONCE SHUNNED (Book #15)
ONCE MISSED (Book #16)
ONCE CHOSEN (Book #17)

MACKENZIE WHITE MYSTERY SERIES
BEFORE HE KILLS (Book #1)
BEFORE HE SEES (Book #2)
BEFORE HE COVETS (Book #3)
BEFORE HE TAKES (Book #4)
BEFORE HE NEEDS (Book #5)
BEFORE HE FEELS (Book #6)
BEFORE HE SINS (Book #7)
BEFORE HE HUNTS (Book #8)
BEFORE HE PREYS (Book #9)
BEFORE HE LONGS (Book #10)
BEFORE HE LAPSES (Book #11)
BEFORE HE ENVIES (Book #12)
BEFORE HE STALKS (Book #13)
BEFORE HE HARMS (Book #14)

AVERY BLACK MYSTERY SERIES
CAUSE TO KILL (Book #1)
CAUSE TO RUN (Book #2)
CAUSE TO HIDE (Book #3)
CAUSE TO FEAR (Book #4)
CAUSE TO SAVE (Book #5)
CAUSE TO DREAD (Book #6)

KERI LOCKE MYSTERY SERIES

Lightning Source UK Ltd.
Milton Keynes UK
UKHW010100170223
417160UK00002B/112